Alice
ALONE

Alice
ALONE

◆

A NOVEL BY
Amanda
Brookfield

St. Martin's Press
New York

Library of Congress Cataloging-in-Publication Data

Brookfield, Amanda.
    Alice alone / Amanda Brookfield.
        p.   cm.
    ISBN 0-312-03276-5
    I. Title.
    PR6052.R58155A79   1989
    823'.914—dc20   89-34976
                                                 CIP

First published in Great Britain by George Weidenfeld and Nicolson Limited.

First U.S. Edition

10 9 8 7 6 5 4 3 2 1

For Mark

Alice
ALONE

· 1 ·

Robin Leaves Home

Alice, a sturdy, steely haired woman of fifty-one, stood on the pavement waving goodbye to the last of her three children to leave home. Robin had grown up more quickly than the first two – probably because of them. Although only nineteen she was already taking the advanced step – or so it seemed to Alice – of throwing herself into the arms of a Birmingham workshop theatre group; and, more specifically, into the hairy arms of its lanky one-earringed director.

The taxi appointed to the historic task of bearing away her youngest daughter to catch the eleven-forty-five from Euston to embark on her new life, had honked its horn outside their door exactly twenty-two minutes ago. Robin, in her usual whirlwind style, had left everything to the last minute. So the morning had been spent in a flurry of ironing, packing and scribbling of phone numbers and addresses for passing on to friends. Only during the final seconds, when she was forced to say something along the lines of a goodbye, did Alice notice the hint of a wobble in her daughter's voice; but it was only a hint and a moment later the cab door slammed shut and Alice was left standing at the gate of No. 12 Quadrant Grove, Belsize Park, waving into thin air.

Like all her friends, Alice's single teenage ambition had

7

been to get married and have a family. A tedious year's secretarial course had secured her a job in a legal firm, which in turn had secured her a husband – in the form of Peter Hatton, a struggling young barrister. They had both been completely inexperienced. Alice because she had only ever got as far as holding a sweaty hand at the end of the occasional party; and Peter because he had been brought up on a closeted nine years at Radley and Oxford. The first of his few attempts at entertaining a girl on his own had nearly put him off women for life. It had been a second cousin who came to his rooms for tea during his final Oxford term. Permission from the Dean and Master of Keble for this momentous event had been secured only on condition that Peter's bed be removed from his room and parked in the corridor for the duration of her visit. The tea itself had not been a wildly successful affair. It was at the instigation of their respective parents that the meeting had been arranged in the first place, and neither found the other particularly interesting or attractive. The obvious removal of the bed (round which Violet had to squeeze her sizeable frame to get to the door of Peter's rooms), did not add to any mood of relaxation. As for Peter, any aptitude he had for small-talk was seriously impeded by an obsessive preoccupation with the idea that if he ever had the nerve to ravage his dumpy cousin, he could just as easily do so on the sofa or the floor. The importance of the bed seemed to him negligible.

Alice had found this an extremely amusing story when Peter first told it to her, as they lay confessing the meagre extent of their respective sexual experiences after a very clumsy first attempt on their honeymoon night. She had laughed, partly from relief that her own lack of expertise did not matter. But she had felt something else too, dimly, and quickly surpressed: a tiny, spontaneous twist of disappointment that Peter was not after all the 'man of the world' that he had till then implied and in which she had taken pleasure in believing. Being good dinner-party

8

material, this story had been repeated by Peter many times since. He usually began: 'I'm sure Alice won't mind if I shock you with the tale of my first encounter with a woman . . .?' and ended, '. . .which taught me never to be shy again!' and other such phrases which implied, falsely, that this inauspicious start had developed into a rollicking bachelorhood. Some dinner-party stories can be introduced again and again, like old friends. This one seemed to Alice to be pulled out like one of Peter's dirty hankies – loved by him, and an object of embarrassment and irritation to her.

They never did become very adept at making love. How the children had been conceived out of a few minutes of self-conscious fumbling on both their parts always struck Alice as a true miracle of nature. But once Simon, then Kate two years later and finally Robin appeared, she had felt utterly contented. It must be easier, she often thought, to have a marriage like theirs, in which the couple make so few demands on each other. There was seldom any question of an argument because they simply did not discuss any topic capable of sparking heated reactions. Peter gave Alice everything she wanted: a comfortable home in North London, plenty of money and the children, whose upbringing he left entirely to her. They ate together, went out together, entertained together and sometimes made love together – about once every three months to be exact. Even on these occasions communication was kept to a minimum. Peter would climb into Alice's bed without saying a word, usually while she was cleaning her teeth. When she returned from the bathroom, he would be lying there quietly, waiting for her, his eyes closed. Long since used to his shyness in these matters, Alice would turn off the light before getting into bed and putting her arms round him. Afterwards he would say 'goodnight, darling' in a gruff, humble way and then slip back between his own sheets on the other side of the bedside table.

She had made the children the sole focus of her life. The

day when they would all finally have left home for good seemed distant, impossible, unthinkable. After Simon had taken a lucrative job as a lawyer in Chicago there had still been Kate and Robin to look after. Then Kate had left to teach at an English school in Madrid; and now Robin, just twenty-two minutes ago, had finally taken herself off to a new life in the Midlands with this Bob Tupper character. For the first time, Alice was alone.

She had watched many of her acquaintances preparing for this same moment in their lives. Coming from perhaps the last generation of non-work-conscious women, few of them had careers to fall back on. Instead they tried to cope with the change by joining book clubs, going to History of Art classes or leaving their husbands. None of these options appealed to Alice. She had hoped, very simply, to be able to heave a long, contented sigh at having done an enjoyable job well; and to spend the rest of her life basking in the afterglow of the achievement, fuelled by memories of earlier days and frequent contact with her offspring. The fallibility of these hazy hopes was quickly becoming apparent. It had been naive and foolish to suppose that by the time the crunch came she would feel old and settled. That was the last thing she felt. Added to that, the careers of Simon and Kate had made keeping in close touch well-nigh impossible. And now Robin – by far the most rebellious and independent of the three – had opted for a frighteningly liberated lifestyle in which Alice knew she could play no part.

They had met Bob once. Robin had brought him home for a weekend a month or so before, in preparation for the earth-shattering news that this was the man with whom she had decided to share her life (marriage not being part of the free social expression on which the theatre workshop was based). Alice had concentrated so hard on trying not to appear shocked by Bob's crew-cut, single earring and obvious physical attraction for her daughter, that she was hardly aware of what the four of them found to say to each

10

other. But her overall impression of him was not favourable. Once he was safely ensconced in his battered Volkswagen van and back on the road to the Midlands she had tried, gently, to talk her daughter out of following him up there a few weeks later. Her motive was a selfless concern for Robin's welfare. Given the choice, she would not have trusted Bob with money for the milkman, let alone the responsibility of looking after her daughter. But when Robin stoutly refused, Alice had felt the first prickings of loneliness; the first anticipation of how she would feel as she turned from waving to the taxi and entered the empty house.

Peter – no doubt, she thought, because he had never allowed himself to feel close to any of his children – had been infuriatingly philosophical about the whole affair. The weekend produced one of the rare occasions on which Alice actually tried to have a discussion with her husband about how she felt. Peter had been as pragmatic as usual and of little comfort.

'Everyone's children go through this stage,' was all the reassurance he offered her. 'Robin will soon get bored with it all – you know what she's like. Anyway, I think it will be good for her to learn to stand on her own two feet. I'd be far more worried if she didn't want to leave home.'

'But Peter, how can you not mind what she's doing? It's almost as if you don't care what happens to her.'

'Don't be ridiculous – of course I care. But we've got to trust her. She's tough enough. If we say no to this plan and to Bob then she'll only go ahead anyway and hate us into the bargain.'

Alice knew that, as ever, his practical view was maddeningly sensible. But the whole business upset her; especially when he said, as he did several times:

'You've got to face it, dear; the children have all grown up now. We have got to get on with our lives and let them get on with theirs.'

It occurred to her – although she never mentioned the

11

fact – that Peter had always done just that anyway. For him there would be no change. He would continue to get up at eight o'clock, eat the breakfast she prepared, sit in the traffic for thirty-five minutes and be at his desk a little after nine. At the weekends he would play golf if the weather was fine and go to his club if it was not. On Sundays he would spend three hours reading the newspapers and then do some work on his book. He was doing some sort of analysis of taxation and company law – Alice could never remember what, exactly. It was two years since he had started working on it and she had long since given up the pretence of showing any interest in the subject or trying to understand what it was all about. The book was simply part of Peter's weekend routine – a routine that only involved her where meals were concerned. If the writing wasn't going well he would spend the evening watching television, making sure he got to bed no later than ten-thirty so as to be fresh for Monday morning. Not having Robin around would not make a scrap of difference to the rhythm of his life.

For Alice it was a different matter. And as she bustled self-consciously round the kitchen, with the sound of the slamming taxi door beating repeatedly inside her head, she was shocked at this new sense of loneliness. It was irrelevant that she had had years to prepare for such a moment. Like waiting for someone to die, the moment when it comes, is still devastating. She felt now what she had always known deep down, but never had to face: that the pleasure in her life had come from making a home for and looking after the children. The fact that, in the process, she had cooked and washed for her husband, had been purely incidental. The full force of this realization made her feel light-headed with panic. As she mechanically scraped the dried egg off the breakfast plates and loaded the washing-up machine, a cold, evil little question kept popping obstinately into her brain: 'What are you going to do now, Alice?' it said; 'What on earth are you going to do now?'

Mercifully, the question was answered, in the short term at least, by the telephone.

'Hello, Alice Hatton speaking.'

'Alice, my dear, how are you? It's Leonie Cordell here, calling after far too long, I know, to ask you and Peter if you would be free for dinner this evening . . . I know it's dreadfully short notice, but you know how we Cordells are – always planning things at the last minute. My dear, do say yes – we'd love to see you both.'

'How very sweet of you, Leonie . . . but I really . . .'

'Geoffrey's just rung from the office to say that he bumped into Peter this morning, who seemed to think that you would both be free . . . We're planning to have some of the trout that Geoffrey caught in Scotland last season – they've been cluttering up my deep-freeze for far too long – so it should be rather a treat for all of us.'

'Yes, well, that sounds wonderful – we're both very fond of trout.' Even as she spoke, Alice secretly marvelled at her ability to sound relatively normal, and to talk sensibly about trout when what she felt like saying was: 'Leonie, Robin has just left home. I feel devastated because I now realize the extent to which I do not love my husband. I feel more like attending a funeral than a dinner party. I don't think I could bear an evening of your prattle . . .'

'Splendid. Shall we say seven? I know it's quite early, but it gives us plenty of time for a few naughty cocktails before dinner. Geoffrey's got some lethal new concoction he wants to try out on us all. Terrible man – I don't know how I've put up with him all these years.' Her voice tailed off into a well-rehearsed tinkle of a laugh, designed to convey enviable matrimonial happiness.

'Until seven, then,' said Alice quickly, sensing that Leonie was in danger of embarking on some dull little confidence about what Geoffrey had said to her recently about her hair, her figure or her face.

'Perfect,' she purred, betraying just a shade of disappointment at having been cut off in mid-flow.

13

Alice dropped the receiver, inwardly cursing Peter for having told Geoffrey that they were free. How dare he not realize that a dinner party with the Cordells was the last thing she would be in the mood for? She considered ringing him, announcing that she refused to go and that he, having got them into it, could damn well get them out of it. But even the idea of a squabble was exhausting, and the dinner did have one thing in its favour. It called for a trip to the hairdresser, thereby taking care of at least some of the long day that stretched ahead.

Unlike many of her contemporaries, Alice was not in the habit of spending several hours each week having her hair, nails, legs 'done'. In fact she found even the relatively simple process of having a shampoo and set – which she normally did once every two weeks or so – rather humiliating. To have her head scrubbed, her hair tweaked into curlers, and then to be stuck under something resembling an old-fashioned space helmet – and, no doubt, twice as uncomfortable – was not her idea of fun. But the result pleased her. Although almost entirely grey, she had an excellent head of thick, healthy hair of which she had always been justly proud.

· 2 ·

The Hairdresser

The receptionist at the hairdresser was clearly put out that Alice had turned up without making an appointment.

'I *think* we can fit you in, though you'll have to wait a bit.'

'That's quite all right,' said Alice politely, 'I'm not in a hurry.'

'And today's Nina's afternoon off, so there's only Gyll or Tony and Gyll's fully booked,' she went on, not without a hint of pleasure, Alice thought. Determined not to be ruffled by the girl's obvious reluctance to make life easy, she said she was sure that Tony would be fine, sat down by the pile of out-of-date, well-thumbed magazines and prepared to wait.

Tony appeared soon enough from a door marked 'Staff Only', smelling strongly of smoke and looking bored. He was a young man of about twenty with a startlingly asymmetrical hairstyle. His appearance did not inspire immediate confidence in his new client.

'You're new here, aren't you?' she asked tentatively.

'As of two weeks ago. A change is as good as a rest they always say. What's it to be, then?'

'Just a wash and set,' said Alice suddenly feeling about a hundred and three. 'It's what I always have,' she added, defensively.

'Nice lot of hair you've got here.' He pulled it back off

15

her face. 'Shame about the colour, though. What about a rinse? It'll take years off you.'

Alice was outraged at the boy's lack of tact. But he had so obviously spoken without meaning to offend – simply saying what he thought – that she felt it would be churlish to take umbrage.

'No, no, really. Just a set as usual, thank you. I don't really approve of dyeing one's hair.'

'Fair enough,' he said amiably and led her off to be scrubbed.

Sitting a few minutes later before the ruthless gaze of the mirror, her wet hair tumbling inelegantly on to her shoulders, Alice dared to consider whether Tony might, after all, be right. She cocked her head to one side and squinted at her reflection. Now that it was wet, her hair looked much darker. It did set off her blue eyes, she decided, drawing attention away from the clusters of wrinkles that surrounded them.

'I wonder,' she said, when Tony reappeared wheeling the trolley of setting equipment; 'I mean, I was thinking about what you said, about having a rinse. Could it be quite a light one – I mean not too dark, but sort of lightish? You see it would be rather a shock after so many years of being grey.'

'Sure it could. No probs with that at all,' he said cheerily. And taking this stumbling request as a firm order, Tony promptly set about changing the colour of Alice's hair. She watched, amazed at her own daring.

Two hours later amazement turned to horror. The curlers were taken out and a totally new head of very dark-brown hair was being bounced into place by Tony's comb.

'I thought you said it wouldn't be too dark,' she stuttered.

'Well, madam, some people's hair takes a lot easier, if you know what I mean. And anyway it could be a lot darker. I think it looks smashing. A new woman,' he added cheekily.

16

Alice, silently believing that 'a lot darker' would have meant jet black, could only smile feebly at the encouragement. She paid the extortionate amount of money to which she had so rashly committed herself and stumbled out into the bright spring sunshine. Never again would she go to that hairdresser, she vowed; and she would live, eat and sleep in a headscarf until all the lovely grey was back in its rightful place.

Thinking of Peter's reaction, her heart missed a beat. He would loathe it. Nothing could be less suitable for a respectably ageing senior barrister's wife than for her to dye her hair all of a sudden. The children though, she thought, would love it. Especially Robin. They were always teasing her about how she should try and look more modern. Occasionally they had even tried buying her bits of modern paste jewellery and patterned tights to 'liven up your image', as Robin would say. Alice had always accepted these well-intentioned gifts with many smiles and promises to wear them 'one day'. But the day never came and they remained safely tucked away at the back of one of her dressing-table drawers.

As she walked home, self-consciously glancing at herself in every shop window, she became aware that her rash decision in the hairdressers was somehow connected with Robin leaving home. She felt neither happier nor less lonely, but at least she had done something. Every glimpse of her strange new appearance was ghastly; but at the same time she felt a little relief at having taken some action by herself, for herself. As for Peter, she thought, it might shock him into . . . Into what she didn't quite know. It will shock him anyway, she concluded, feeling a twinge of childish excitement at the sense of having done something so utterly disgraceful.

She hurriedly let herself into their large Victorian house, terrified of being spotted by the neighbours. Since they were not even on sugar-lending terms, they would have been unlikely to comment to her face. It was the sniggering behind curtains of which she was afraid. The complete emptiness of the house, without the presence or the prospect of Robin, echoed at her as she slammed the front door. They had normally eaten lunch together. Robin's drama and dance classes had only been a short bus ride away in Camden Town, and four days out of five she would nip home for a snack and a chat.

Realizing now that it was after three o'clock and that she had not eaten since breakfast, Alice peered into the fridge to see if anything could tempt her appetite. The cold lamb – left over from the special 'farewell' dinner she had cooked the night before – looked tired and grey. That and the thought of dinner with the Cordells dissolved her hunger. She recalled that Leonie used her dinner parties as an excuse to break the rules of every diet – and there were many – that she had ever been on. They would be lucky to get away with less than four courses, not to mention bowls of crisps and peanuts to go with the cocktails. Alice shuddered to think of it. She shut the fridge door and went upstairs to change the sheets in Robin's room and give it a good clean, so that it would be ready for her whenever she decided to return.

· 3 ·

First Reactions

To concentrate on expecting the worst is a popular way of hoping to be pleasantly surprised. Alice tried this trick with regard to both Peter's reaction to her new appearance and dinner with the Cordells. It failed to work on both counts.

Peter Hatton was in excellent spirits as he dodged his smart, silver BMW through the evening rush hour. He had arranged to play golf at the weekend with one of his richest clients and the balmy April evening promised the start of a long-awaited spell of good weather. What is more, he was thoroughly looking forward to an indulgent few hours of eating and drinking with the Cordells. As he swung into the peaceful cul-de-sac of Quadrant Grove, he made a mental note to ask Alice to drive home afterwards. It was near the end of another busy week and he felt like letting himself go a bit.

'Anyone home?' he shouted, with uncharacteristic joviality, as he dumped his briefcase in the hall and began flicking through the day's post.

'I'm in the bath,' called back Alice. 'Shall I leave the water in?' She was on the point of saying that she hadn't washed her hair in it, so it was quite clean, but thought better of bringing up the subject of hair just yet.

'If you haven't washed your hair in it – yes please,' yelled Peter, unaware of his extraordinary powers of telepathy. 'It will save time.'

She heard him padding up the stairs and into their bedroom, which adjoined the bathroom. She slipped lower amongst the bath-suds, in defensive anticipation of his appearance.

'Did Robin get off all right?' he called through the open door. 'Apparently lots of trains from Euston were buggered up this morning because of a go-slow or something – at least that was Denise's excuse for being late,' he chuckled.

'Yes, fine, I think. At least she didn't call from the station, so it must have been OK. Anyway, Denise always seems to be arriving late on some pretext or other.'

Denise was a scatter-brained trainee barrister whom Peter's firm had just taken on to do her pupillage and for whom Peter appeared to have rather a soft spot.

'Yes, and for such a bright girl she really does have rather an unimaginative line in excuses,' he said, laughing again.

This smooth exchange of pleasantries between man and wife was brought to an abrupt conclusion by Peter's entrance into the bathroom.

'Good God, Alice, what have you done?' he gasped, staring at her in horror.

Until this point, Alice had been feeling genuinely contrite – quite ready to be the first to admit her folly and explain that the new boy Tony had underestimated how well her hair would 'take', with apologies and promises to grow it out and never to try such a rash experiment again. But the gawping, incredulous face of her husband immediately removed any inclination to go through her rehearsed list of excuses.

'What does it look as if I've done?' she retorted, getting out of the bath and reaching for a towel.

'Will it wash out?' he asked, still looking as if someone had plunged a knife into his stomach.

'Of course it won't wash out – it's *dyed*'; she lingered sadistically on the final word, watching the effect on his agonized expression.

'But *why*, Alice? You've always said you hated dyed hair,'

– he could hardly bring himself to utter the words – 'and
. . . and leg-shaving and all those things. You think they're
unnatural –or you used to think so . . .' He glanced quickly
at her legs as he spoke.

'Don't be ridiculous,' she said, instinctively hiding her
still unshaven legs with the bath towel. 'I . . . I . . . just felt
like a change, that's all. I was a bit shocked too, at first, but
now I like it. Yes I really like it,' she said, looking at herself
defiantly in the mirror.

'I don't believe this', Peter muttered, reaching aggressively for his razor and almost knocking her out of the way as
he did so. Spraying lavish amounts of *L'Homme* shaving
foam onto his cheeks, he went on: 'And have you – did you –
stop to consider even for a second what people will think?'

Standing a little behind him, still wrapped in the bath
towel, Alice ignored his question. Arms crossed and
frowning, she continued to stare challengingly at his
reflection in the mirror, waiting for him to finish.

'I'll tell you what people will think . . .'

'I thought you might,' she whispered, bracing herself.

'. . . They will think that your menopausal crisis is such
that you have resorted to the crudest, most clichéd method
in existence of clinging on to your lost youth. You will
therefore appear ridiculous.'

The cruelty of his words surprised even Peter. The
Hattons were not used to arguing. In all the twenty-six
years they had been married, their shared moments of
extreme feeling – whether of pleasure or unhappiness –
could be counted on the fingers of one hand. They moved
through life side by side, neither touching nor crossing
each other's paths. Neither did they have an established
language or ritual for arguing. They were fighting with
entirely new weapons, discovering for the first time how
sharp they could be.

Alice was far more deeply hurt than her anger or her
pride would allow her to show. Her reply was in a cold,
brittle tone that Peter had never heard before.

21

'I rather feel,' she said icily, 'that someone who is in danger of losing all his hair, not to mention losing his belt buckle in the folds of his stomach, should be the one to stop and consider how he might set about regaining such youthful attractiveness as he ever possessed.' Even as she spoke, she was aware that, unlike most occasions when the right words only come to mind afterwards, her hurt pride and her anger had inspired the perfect articulation of her thoughts. But then the moment of inspiration died. 'And anyway, I didn't do it to look younger, I just wanted to look a little different, that's all,' she ended weakly.

'You'd better get ready – we're going to be late,' was all he said in return.

As they took their seats in the BMW, the Hattons both felt acutely unhappy. But just as they had no established pattern of argument, so they had no ritual of reconciliation to fall back on either. They drove in a thick silence, Alice's mind blank with despair and Peter's focusing firmly on the approaching relief of a strong drink.

· 4 ·

The Dinner Party

The Hattons had known the Cordells for years, but only as dinner-party acquaintances. As far as Alice was concerned, all their friends fell into this category. Peter might play golf or work with the husbands, but she rarely saw the wives on her own – except for the odd occasion on which she was forced to help out with some or other charity fund-raising event. This suited her very well. She did not like other women very much – especially not on their own. Throughout her life – from school to secretarial college to marriage – Alice had always prefered to socialize amongst a large group of people whom she quite liked, but did not depend on. Generally this system worked smoothly; many pleasant dinner parties were given and had, with each side respecting the level of polite friendliness on which the relationship was based. With a couple like the Cordells, however, things were a little less satisfactory. Geoffrey was all right. But his wife was one of those ladies who fancied herself as everybody's Closest Friend. That all her acquaintances suffered the same treatment made it no easier to tolerate.

It would be untrue to say that Leonie did not bat an eyelid at the sight of Alice when she swung open their shiny, pine front door. She did blink and hesitate, but only for a split second. She then quickly made up for it with a torrential welcome of delight, congratulation, appreciation and every other positive sentiment – except love of course – known to man.

'How absolutely marvellous you look! When did you . . . well fancy keeping such a tremendous secret from me . . . but what a lovely surprise too! You can hardly have recognized her, Peter . . . oh, I love it, Alice, I really love it! But look at me, keeping you on the doorstep like this – come in, come in, give me your coats . . . No coats? No, of course not with this lovely weather – silly me. Now please go on through – I'll just see how Geoffrey's getting on with that wicked, wicked cocktail of his. Won't be a tick.'

Leonie glided rapidly into the kitchen, shutting the door behind her. Geoffrey was standing at the breakfast bar, measuring jugfuls of various spirits and fruit juices into a large mixing bowl, sticking his tongue out in concentration as he did so.

'Geoffrey, listen – stop that a sec. They've arrived.'

'I know they've arrived, which is why I'm not going to stop because they will be waiting for a drink.' He spoke slowly and deliberately, concentrating hard on the job in hand. 'Do you think you could cut up some fruit and cucumber and things to float on the top?' he asked, 'it always looks much nicer like that, don't you think?'

'Yes, Geoffrey darling, it always looks much nicer with things floating in it and I'll cut up the entire contents of the fruit bowl in just a minute, but first I must warn you . . .' She glanced quickly over her shoulder to check the door was firmly shut and Geoffrey, catching a note of real urgency in his wife's voice, put down the bottle of vodka he held and looked up enquiringly.

'It's Alice, darling, she's dyed her hair completely black –well, a sort of very dark brown anyway – and it looks rather startling. I thought I'd tell you as she does look different – quite hideous in fact – and, it wouldn't do for you to look too astounded.' She giggled. 'Poor Peter looks positively storming,' – Leonie, for all her prattling, could be quite perceptive on occasions – 'he's such a square old stick, he must loathe it. I wonder what made her do it? I mean Alice isn't exactly one for the latest fashions, is she? Perhaps she's got her eye on a younger man . . . ooh, what a scandal that would be!' She rolled her eyes gleefully at such a deliciously wicked idea.

Geoffrey returned his attentions to the bottle of vodka and the mixing bowl. Secretly he wondered why the dyeing of Alice's hair should seem such a scandal to his wife, who had for years relied on the peroxide powers of a product called 'Blonde Beauty'. Sensing however, that the expression of such a view would not be greeted with much enthusiasm, he contented himself with saying:

'I'll be discretion itself, I promise. And after a few swigs of this I shouldn't think old Peter will feel too badly about it either.' He gave the deadly yellow liquid a final stir, patted Leonie on the bottom and set off to welcome his guests.

There was no sound coming from the huge room into which Leonie had ushered Peter and Alice. In fact the silence was so obvious and embarrassing that Geoffrey felt tempted to start whistling as he approached, to give them fair warning of his arrival. Instead he marched boldly in, saying: 'Welcome! Welcome!' before he had even set eyes on either of them. The Hattons stood up self-consciously.

'Alice, lovely to see you – you look . . . magnificent . . . as always,' he said, groping for inspiration. Turning quickly to Peter, he shook him warmly by the hand. 'Long time no see, eh?' He knew he sounded too hearty and wondered why his lovely, newly refurbished lounge suddenly felt like a morgue.

Just then Leonie came sailing in through the open door, bearing the mixing bowl – now with bits floating in it – triumphantly before her.

'The moment all you poor thirsty people have been waiting for!', she proclaimed. They smiled at her weakly, but with unanimous relief.

'Alice, be a dear and clear a bit more space on the table for me . . . oh, Geoffrey darling, we've forgotten the crispy

25

nibbles – they're on the side in the kitchen . . . Peter, you couldn't reach up there for those little cocktail glasses could you?' So Leonie, with well-practised, sugary skill, marshalled them all into activity. They each fell thankfully to their duties and shortly found themselves settled almost naturally amongst the deep folds and chintz cushions of the Cordell's three-piece suite. There followed an energetic and detailed discussion of Geoffrey's aptitude for mixing cocktails and Leonie's astonishing expertise when it came to dips.

But the alcohol, as if recognizing its task, was soon racing efficiently round their bloodstreams. Peter and Geoffrey took off their ties and began to talk about golf. Alice and Leonie, after a short discussion about hairdressers, disappeared into the kitchen, where Leonie confided at great length that, having lost four pounds in two days by eating nothing but peanuts, she was planning on indulging herself to the full. When they returned to the sitting room Leonie gratified herself and infuriated Alice by flirtatiously implying that they had been exchanging the most intimate of secrets about their husbands. Fortunately both Geoffrey and Peter seemed far more intent on emptying the contents of the mixing bowl than in playing the outraged husband game with Leonie. Once they had accomplished this, the Cordells led their guests through to take their seats at an enormous mock-medieval dining-room table, upon which four platefuls of asparagus mousse wobbled expectantly.

'And how's that lovely daughter of yours? Still keeping herself out of mischief I hope,' said Geoffrey to Alice some time later.

'Actually she's just left home to go and live in Birmingham,' she replied, trying to sound bright and nonchalant about the event that had shattered the entire pattern of her life.

'It must be a man, it always is,' squealed Leonie, whose train of thought on any subject was invariably the same.

'Yes, she does in fact have a boyfriend up there,' said

Alice, hating the feel of Leonie's lascivious imagination going to work on the life of her daughter.

'But the main reason she's flown the nest,' she went on, trying her best to sound enthusiastic and pleased, 'is to go and work with a very interesting theatre group who happen to be based in Birmingham. She wants to be an actress, you see.'

At this point, Peter – his face now saggy and flushed with alcohol – burst out laughing.

'You're absolutely right, Leonie, because what my wife has for some reason failed to mention is that Robin's boyfriend runs the theatre group – so the two are very much part of the same deal, as it were. Alice doesn't like him, do you, darling? But he seems very fond of Robbie and that's good enough for me.'

Alice looked down at her plate. The goggling eye of a trout returned her gaze from a lush bed of curly green lettuce.

'Oh Peter, I do believe you're almost as romantic as Geoffrey,' chimed Leonie, ostentatiously winking at her husband who, since his nose was busy exploring the bouquet of the Chablis he had just distributed, was the only member of the party who failed to notice the gesture.

'Mmmmm,' he said instead, his eyes closed as he inhaled deeply, 'I really do recommend this one, Peter. Tell me what you think.'

'No! No! Stop!,' shrieked Leonie. 'Let's propose a toast and all drink together. Now hang on . . . Oh, I've got it. Right, here we go.' She cleared her throat importantly. 'Let's drink to Peter and Alice and their new, childless freedom.' She beamed at them as she raised her glass. 'Here's to your second honeymoon and the best years of your lives!'

Alice felt sick. Any minute now, she thought, I'm going to scream. They all chinked glasses clumsily.

''Spose your marriage's been one long honeymoon then,' slurred Peter, 'not having had any children.' He tried to give Geoffrey a knowing look. The result was a rather strange contortion which he then seemed to have trouble removing from his face. Thus occupied, he was too engrossed to notice that his words caused the first glimpse of genuine feelings to pass like dark clouds across the features of his hosts. Alice saw only too clearly. For a brief second she felt truly sorry for the childless Cordells. Normally, whether out of compassion or sheer politeness, she would have waded in to try and help them all. But the sense of being so utterly alone with her own newly discovered pain made her selfish. Taking a tiny, slow sip of her wine, merely allowing the cool dry taste to wet her lips, she eyed Leonie from over the rim of her glass, wondering how she would react.

'If you've all finished, I'll get the cheese,' said Leonie, leaving Geoffrey to assure Peter that not having children was the key to utter contentment.

The first two courses had been so plentiful that Peter mistook the appearance of the cheese board for the final stage of the meal. He made a greedy assault on no less than four of the five cheeses on offer, took two more biscuits than he felt he should and even treated himself to second helpings of the brie, which was mouth-wateringly soft and deceptively light. He was on the point of asking Geoffrey if he had any good cigars in the house when Leonie reappeared from another sortie to the kitchen bearing an enormous bowl of chocolate mousse, decorated with generous dollops of double cream.

'This is Geoffrey's favourite pud in the whole world, isn't it, darling? I sometimes think you married me for my chocolate mousse,' she giggled coquettishly.

'I was indeed blinded by your chocolate mousse, my love' said her husband, a slight edge in his voice. 'But seriously, it is excellent, so forget your waistlines and tuck in.'

Leonie stole a conspiratorial glance at Alice, who pretended not to notice. Peter secretly loosened his belt by one hole, using his large damask napkin as cover for the operation.

Leonie insisted on serving the mousse rather than allowing them to help themselves, which meant that everyone got more than they actually wanted – except for Leonie, who unashamedly had seconds as well.

'A little cream in your coffee, Peter?', she asked, once they had all heaved themselves back into the sitting room. Peter, who felt that one more drop of cholesterol, in any form, would trigger an immediate and massive heart attack, politely declined.

'What a delicious dinner, Leonie. Thank you so much – it's such a treat not to have to cook for a change,' said Alice, sneaking a look at her watch to see if they had reached an acceptable hour for departure. It was nearly midnight. Peter had miraculously refused several invitations to treat himself to a liqueur, which meant they were just two swigs of his coffee away from release.

'Now that Robin's gone, we really must see more of each other, Alice. I've forgotten, do you play bridge?'

'No,' said Alice, a shade too quickly, 'and I really feel I'm too old to learn.'

'My dear, don't be ridiculous. All of us are trillions of years away from being old, aren't we boys?'

Stifling a burp, Geoffrey agreed heartily and Peter, whose head had been falling onto his chest, turned the movement into vigorous nod of assent.

'But Alice,' Leonie persisted, 'what on earth will you do with your days now that you don't have Robin to rush round for and look after? It must feel like such a change.' Her voice was a little breathless with excitement. She was dying for Alice to confess that she was miserable and lonely. Not because she really wanted to help, nor because she wanted the flattery of being selected as a confidante. No, what Leonie was after was the secret thrill that comes with hearing of someone's misfortunes; the same wicked pleasure that forces a smile to the lips at the news of a

29

terrible disaster. Leonie thrived on such moments. They made her feel lucky and strong. Outwardly she would switch on the taps of compassion and solace. Inwardly she would relish that delicious tingle of being privy to, but safe from, real unhappiness.

'Yes, of course it is an enormous change,' said Alice, abruptly getting up from the sofa and reaching for her handbag. 'But I've so many things I want to get on with that I am really looking forward to it. And now, Peter, we really must say our farewells and let Leonie and Geoffrey get some sleep.'

They drove home in silence; Alice at the wheel, Peter noisily fighting off indigestion beside her. The image of Leonie spooning chocolate mousse into her mouth as she made eyes at the two drunken men sitting opposite her kept forming in Alice's mind. She had felt a world apart from all three of them, as if they had been performing in some farcical play in which she had no role. What depressed her most was that this feeling of isolation came from an unhappiness against which she was defenceless; and which was likely to get worse with time, not better. For without her children and without love for her husband she had lost all sense of the part she was supposed to be playing in life. She was in limbo and she was on her own.

· 5 ·

Alice Protests

The next morning, for the first time in twenty-six years, Alice decided not to get out of bed when the alarm went off. This meant that Peter would not have his morning cup of tea in bed, nor be able to rely on the delicious smell of coffee and toast as an incentive to drag himself into the bathroom. She lay with her back towards him, waiting for the radio alarm to crackle into life and wondering how he would react.

Peter, as yet blissfully unaware of the fate that awaited him, was dreaming vividly about Denise. She had just sat on his desk and started running her long cool fingers through his hair – hair which, for the purposes of the dream, was miraculously plentiful – when the telephone rang. The moment of intimacy was ruined. No matter how many times he picked up and put down the receiver, it kept on ringing. Gradually the noise transformed itself into Big Ben chiming eight o'clock, courtesy of Radio 4. Feeling disappointed, rather hung-over, but also slightly guilty, Peter waited to hear the familiar rustle of Alice slipping out of bed and the welcome creaking of the stairs which meant she was going to put the kettle on. After a few minutes he reached out and turned the radio up a little, with the aim of waking her from what he judged to be an unusually deep sleep. Then he coughed loudly. Alice lay motionless, suppressing a schoolgirl urge to burst into a fit of nervous giggles.

'Alice,' said Peter at last, 'are you awake?' It had already crossed his mind as a serious possibility that she might be dead.

'Yes, I've been awake for ages,' she said, burrowing further under the bed clothes.

'It's already eight fifteen, you know.'

'Yes I know.' She was almost beginning to enjoy herself.

'Well, aren't you going to get up?'

'No, Peter, I honestly don't think I am – not just yet, anyway.'

Peter was genuinely astounded. Then furious. She knew he had trouble remembering where the sugar bowl lived, let alone being capable of cooking his own breakfast. His one attempt, many years previously, to treat her to breakfast in bed, when he had left the egg in the water for four and a half minutes but forgotten to turn the stove on, was another one of his favourite after-dinner stories. He chose to contain his wrath only for the simple reason that he was by now quite worried about his wife's state of mind. Indeed, the more he thought about it, the more peculiar Alice's recent behaviour seemed to be. First there had been her extraordinary decision to opt for an odious new hair colour, which she had then defended with uncharacteristic venom; then her curt replies and bristly silences through-out the evening at the Cordells had been positively embarrassing; and now there was this equally uncharacter-istic attack of apathy.

'Are you feeling all right?'

'I feel fine. But I don't feel like getting out of bed.' She wanted to add, 'because there's nothing to get out of bed for,' but thought better of it.

At a complete loss, Peter shuffled off to the bathroom. He knew that women of Alice's age got depressed because of complicated things to do with hormone changes and the menopause, but Alice had long since had a hysterectomy, which at the time had hardly seemed to bother her at all. He wondered if it wasn't just worry about Robin that was

32

behind it all. Both the Hattons were so used to getting on with their own lives without showing any emotional dependence on each other that Peter, even when he had decided that anxiety about the welfare of their daughter must be the reason for Alice's strange behaviour, felt awkward about trying to reassure her. Resolving stoically not to mention his distress at having to forgo breakfast – it was now too late for him to do battle with the kettle and the toaster himself – he returned to the bedroom and tried to say something helpful.

'You shouldn't worry about Robin, you know. She's more than capable of looking after herself,' he ventured at last. Adjusting his tie in the mirror, he watched the reflection of the bundle of bedclothes to see if this display of sympathy prompted them to move at all.

'I'm not worried about Robin,' came Alice's muffled voice. 'No,' she thought, 'it's not Robin I'm worried about, it's me.' But the idea of trying to explain any of her panic to Peter simply did not seem worthwhile. Too many years had gone by during which she had never reached out to him for emotional support – nor he to her – and the gap between them was now too wide to bridge. The words 'I don't love you or even like you very much and you are all I've got,' formed themselves in her mind, but the idea of saying them was impossible. Perhaps if Alice had felt that she had an option – a lover to run to, a sick mother who needed nursing or a private income on which she could support herself – then she might have had the courage to start to try and tell the truth. Instead she said: 'I'm afraid you'll have to buy a bacon sandwich or something on the way to work.'

Peter was unused to feeling quite so much at a loss as to how to respond to a situation. He felt it was unfair of Alice to start playing such games with him. It made him impatient and annoyed – as did anything that he could not understand. He made one last attempt to summon his wife out of her strange, new lethargy:

'Why don't we go out somewhere together tonight . . .

give ourselves a treat? How about that for a good idea?' His gaiety was so forced that Alice once again felt the childish compulsion to burst out laughing.

'OK,' she replied, after a deep breath and a long pause, and without quite the enthusiasm Peter had been hoping for.

'Right then. I'll get Glenda to fix up theatre tickets and book a table. I'll meet you . . . let's see . . . outside Green Park tube station at seven-thirty. That should be safe enough.'

'Fine,' said Alice, now sitting up in bed, looking – as Peter couldn't help registering – very tired and dishevelled. Her smart new hair-do was sticking out at chaotic angles and traces of mascara made the circles under her eyes appear darker than they actually were.

She continued to sit there, propped like an invalid amongst the pillows, long after Peter had given her a hasty farewell peck on the cheek. The familiar noises that accompanied his daily exit from the house grated on her nerves. This morning all those routine slamming, clanking and revving sounds had a sinister echo, as if they were laughing at her despair. For it was indeed despair that Alice now felt. Not only the day, but the week, the year, her entire life stretched blankly before her. She stared mindlessly at the wall opposite. Its garlands of pink and yellow roses blurred as her eyes began to water from the strain of not blinking. Their busy bright colours seemed to hold more promise of happiness than anything her life had to offer. Her eyes were smarting badly, but she was not crying, nor did she feel capable of doing so. It was as if fear of an enormous vacuum in which she now found herself had shocked her into a motionless silence – the sort of silence that comes from being too terrified even to scream. Then, into the dreadful quiet of the house and her mind, dropped the same cold, hard voice that had taunted her the previous morning: 'What are you going to do?' it said, 'What on earth are you going to do?'

She threw herself out of bed, pulled on some clothes and began a frenzy of activity about the house. She polished the already glistening parquet, sorted out immaculately tidy drawers and scrubbed the gleaming surfaces in the kitchen and bathroom. Then she went shopping and bought huge amounts of food they could never eat and stocked up on all the cleaning sprays, waxes and foams that already lined the shelves of her broom cupboad. It was still only four o'clock. So she then copied all her handwritten recipes into a new notebook and wrote the birthdays of every friend and relation she could think of into the diary – even though she had to guess most of the dates. To get her round to six o'clock she filled in all the engagements and events since January that had not been recorded in the diary, ending up with 'Robin leaves home.' She was going to put in the dinner with the Cordells and her prospective meal with Peter, but something stopped her. Not a dramatically defiant feeling; just an absolute sense that from the day that Robin had left, the incidents making up the pattern of her life had ceased to have any value or significance.

· 6 ·

Waiting for Peter

Alice looked at her watch for the hundredth time since she had arrived, punctual almost to the second, at Green Park Tube station. The minute hand had crawled round a couple more millimetres and now read eight-fifteen. Peter was inclined to be late, but not this late. She decided to wait until eight-thirty and then go home. When eight-thirty arrived, she resolved to give him just fifteen more minutes.

It crossed her mind that he might have had an accident. Closing her eyes in concentration, she tried to imagine how she would feel if Peter died, but she couldn't make it seem real. Her mind resorted to clichéd images of echoing hospital corridors, saline drips and romantic bedside re-conciliations. Whereas she knew that, in reality, trying to cope with such a death-bed scene would be far more likely to embarrass than unite them. They would both find the free play of all those raw, unsubtle feelings of fear, regret and compassion intolerable. Nor did Alice allow herself to fantasize that the timely exit of her husband would answer any of her newly discovered problems. She was wise enough to recognize that, without Peter beside her, she would be more vulnerable than ever. Armies of cause-seeking Leonie Cordells would come marching into Quadrant Grove demanding the right to be involved in her life. It was a prospect even more horrifying than living, as she did now, with the sense that her once-fulfilling role had dissolved into nothing. At least with Peter around she could guard her desolation, and her pride, behind the semblance of a secure married life.

Her reverie was interrupted by a tap on the shoulder. She spun round, ready with an indigant 'and where have you been.' But it was not Peter. It was a policeman. Her first thought was that he had come to tell her that there had been an accident.

'Everything all right is it, madam?' The sharpness in his voice caught Alice by surprise.

She stared at him blankly, noting that he looked several years younger than Robin. The observation did not help to take the edge out of her own voice.

'Yes, of course everything's all right, thank you, constable. I'm just waiting for someone.'

'Pleased to hear it. It's just that I couldn't help noticing that you'd been standing here rather a long time, madam. I wondered if you might be requiring help of any sort.' He didn't look or sound as if he had the slightest intention of offering any help and spoke with a bored impatience that Alice found intensely insulting.

'I've been waiting for my husband,' she said haughtily. 'He must have been delayed at the office. In fact I was on the point of phoning him to find out what has happened.'

'That sounds like a very good idea, madam,' he said sarcastically, looking over her shoulder and tapping his foot. He continued to stand there, obviously waiting for her to go.

Alice was so outraged that she strode off without thinking what direction she was taking. So much for the friendly bobby she fumed, stomping along noisily and somewhat precariously on her stilettos, cursing Peter and the entire metropolitan police force under her breath as she went. Too furious to care where she was heading, she turned down towards Shepherd Market, looking around all the time for a phone box. It struck her after a while that it would be wise to retrace her steps and use the phones in the tube station, but she could not face the prospect of walking all the way back or of running into the same loathsome policeman. What right had he, she thought again, to 'move her on' like that. Since when had it been a criminal offence to wait for someone. . . She stopped suddenly. Not because she had at last seen a phone box, but because a terrible thought occurred to her. It was incredible, but just possible that that officious adolescent had actually suspected her of . . . of. . . Alice couldn't even think of the word for a moment . . . of soliciting, she finally thought, almost saying it out loud. The idea was ludicrous but not impossible. Feeling quite shaky, she set off again, turning into an attractive little alleyway at the end of which gleamed the lights of what looked like a small bistro.

If it hadn't been so dark, Alice might have caught a glimpse of herself in one of the windows she passed and seen that the young policeman could almost have been forgiven for suspecting her motives for hanging round Green Park Tube station for well over an hour.

The hairdresser had managed to make Alice's new hair colour look quite elegant by shaping it into a gentle but immaculate bob. The result had been modern, yet safely classic. Unfortunately her own attempt at using a combination of heated rollers and a hair-dryer in order to achieve a similar effect had not met with the same success. Some of the curls that were meant to curve neatly inwards, giving the smart straight line of the bob, obediently did so. But the majority had been far more rebellious. The unhappy consequence was that it looked as if Alice had spent many hours trying to make her hair fall into a wild assemblage of curls in order to look younger; whilst the lines on her face clearly indicated that the rich chestnut colour almost certainly came out of a bottle. She was also wearing too much make-up in an attempt to hide the dark bags and pastiness brought on by lack of sleep; and her evening lipstick was bright red. It matched the flowers on her dress, but as her coat was buttoned up and the flowers hidden, this fact was not evident. The grey mackintosh was scruffier than the rest of the outfit, and could have been interpreted – by someone on the lookout for such clues – as an attempt to cover up a too-glamorous dress. But gathering rain clouds had called for something, both umbrellas were in the car and it was the only waterproof coat that she possessed. Such an appearance, combined with an apparently pointless stay in the garish lights at the entrance to Green Park Tube and a young policeman who over-estimated his own powers of perception, meant that Alice's suspicions about why she was 'moved on' were entirely correct.

Once inside the bistro she was welcomed by a pert, olive-skinned waiter and a mouth-watering smell of garlic and roasting meat. Refusing the offer of a table, she asked if she might use a telephone. He amiably showed her to a pay-phone situated in an ill-lit corridor next to the toilets.

After the machine had swallowed three of Alice's four ten pence pieces, she was rewarded with the voice of a very worried and, initially, contrite-sounding Peter.

'Alice, thank goodness you've called. I'm so sorry about the mess-up, but a last-minute crisis descended on us just as I was leaving the office. I tried to call home, but you must have already left. Why on earth didn't you call earlier?'

'Because I was waiting at Green Park Tube station,' she retorted icily, marvelling at the way he had moved rapidly from an apology to an implication that she was partly to blame.

'Yes, well, I'm extremely sorry, dear – we'll have to make up for it tomorrow night.'

Alice didn't say anything.

'Are you all right? Where are you calling from?'

Alice wondered how Peter would react if she told him that she had just been mistaken for a whore.

'Oh yes, I'm fine, thanks,' she said with deliberate sarcasm. 'I'm calling from a restaurant.'

'What on earth are you doing in a restaurant?'

At this point the pips went.

'I haven't any more change. . .'

'Damn, right I'll get home as soon as. . .'

The line went dead. As Alice made her way back into the crowded bistro, the olive-skinned waiter caught sight of her and asked if she would now be requiring a table. On impulse and astounding herself, Alice said that yes, she would. He promptly led her to the one free table and politely pulled back a chair for her to sit down. It was laid for two and decorated with a smart red and white checked tablecloth and a vase containing a single red carnation.

It was the first time in her entire life that Alice had sat down in a restaurant to eat alone. She ordered a gin and tonic, snails in garlic butter, steak au poivre, and a half bottle of the house red. The whole situation seemed completely unreal. She didn't feel like Alice Hatton at all. In fact, she felt totally separated from her surroundings – as if her mind had somehow detached itself from her body and was now coolly watching her actions to see what she did next.

Just as she was grappling with the first snail, whose shell was coated in such a generous amount of garlicky butter that it kept slipping infuriatingly out of the special tongs supplied for the operation, a strange man tapped her on the shoulder for the second time that evening.

'Excuse me. I'm so sorry to interrupt, but your table has the only spare place in the entire restaurant. If you're not expecting anyone, I would love to make use of it – I'm absolutely ravenous. I promise to be very quiet and not bother you at all.' He was already pulling back the chair and Alice had little option but to murmur her assent. She concentrated hard on her snails.

'Those look good. I think I'll have the same.'

'Yes . . . yes they are delicious – if you like garlic that is,' she added timidly.

'Love the stuff – even if it is, shall we say, a little

unsociable.' He laughed as he said this, clearly very much at ease. When the waiter returned to take his order, it became clear that he was a regular customer.

'I'll have the snails tonight, Pablo – with lots of garlic mind you – followed by, let's see now . . . yes, the steak au poivre cooked 'a punto' and a bottle of the usual.'

'Just like madam,' said Pablo with a knowing wink. Alice nearly dissolved with embarrassment.

'So you've ordered the same – what a coincidence,' he said easily. 'Good choice, I can assure you. Their steaks are always excellent.'

Alice was in two minds as to how she should cope with the situation. On the one hand she felt awkward, utterly disorientated and desperate to escape. But at the same time she felt free – albeit in a disembodied sort of way – and rather curious to find out more about her companion. Shortly after he sat down a couple from a nearby table got up and left but he made no offer to move. His smiling face also made it plain that he was quite open to the idea of striking up a conversation with her.

Perhaps it was the gin and tonic on an empty stomach. Perhaps it was the tangy house red; or the couple of glasses of beautifully smooth Auberge de something or other that he ordered. Whatever it was, Alice found herself in the wholly unexpected position of feeling more relaxed and happy than she had for months. To begin with she battled against the dreadful temptation to tell him all about herself. The idea of off-loading all her secret confusion and misery onto a completely objective, but probably quite sympathetic stranger was very appealing. Not only would it be a relief to pour it all out, but she sensed too that it would be curiously unembarrassing and easy – simply because he knew nothing of her life or the people in it.

But she resisted. They talked instead about snails, then frogs' legs, which somehow led onto deep-sea diving, which took them to yachting, the Bahamas, skin cancer, doctors, ending up with a quick dip into euthanasia – just as the coffee was being served.

'I'd like to be able to choose when I'm switched off,' he said lightly, 'though I suppose if I'm converted into a speechless, tube-riddled vegetable by some gruesome accident I won't exactly have much say in the matter.' As with so much that he had said, he made it sound funny and Alice found herself laughing in spite of the subject-matter. For the third or fourth time that evening she wondered how old he was. His dark beard was streaked with grey and his face was heavily lined and leathery, suggesting many years of exposure to a hot sun. But his eyes, set perhaps a little too close together, she thought, had a youthful spark of mischief and his voice was rich and energetic. Forty-six maybe? She looked again. He could just as easily have been fifty-six. Whatever he was, she was extremely pleased to have met him. This sudden influx of pleasure into her life and adrenalin into her blood made her cheeks glow and her pulse race. By the time they got to the coffee and the euthanasia discussion she was floating on air. She wanted the evening to go on for ever. Peter, Quadrant Grove, the Cordells, loneliness – all had become blurred images and hazy memories at the back of her mind. How could they ever have mattered, she wondered euphorically, giving her dinner companion yet another of her beaming smiles. In fact her face ached from all the smiling and laughing she had been doing.

'I wouldn't mind a nightcap,' she blurted out recklessly; and then was all at once terrified that he would look shocked or, worse still, refuse the offer.

'Excellent idea,' came the immediate reply, 'but let's not stay here. My club is just round the corner. Why don't we go there instead?'

Alice could only grin her assent, the capacity for speech having mysteriously deserted her. He insisted on paying the bill and gave her his arm as they left the restaurant – which was just as well, as she found herself feeling quite giddy from the combination of pleasure and too much wine. The realization – brought on by the dizziness when she stood up – that she had had rather too much to drink did not bother her at all. Nor did she feel the slightest embarrassment or offence when Pablo shot her companion a final parting wink.

As they strolled the couple of hundred yards to Langtons Club, their paces falling naturally into rhythm, the air seemed strangely fresh and quiet for London. Alice felt as if she was in another world entirely; a world in which she wasn't Alice Hatton, but some new powerful creature for whom anything was possible.

'My goodness,' she suddenly burst out, her voice sounding disturbingly loud in the silence of the night, 'I've just this second realized – I don't even know your name. . .'

He chuckled, 'But names don't really matter in situations like this, do they?'

'No, no I suppose they don't,' she whispered, feeling, with this wonderful discovery of a new self, as if she knew exactly what he meant.

'Tell you what though,' he went on teasingly, 'I'll be Horatio – as in Nelson – and you can be. . .'

'Lady Hamilton!' she put in triumphantly, feeling daring yet entirely natural. He too was acting as if the events of the evening were the most normal thing in the world. It was sensing this that fuelled her own confidence in what she was doing.

The main sitting room of the club was full of people. Lounging in the vast armchairs and sofas was the usual smattering of timeless old gentlemen puffing on cigars and nursing indigestion. In one corner a rowdy party of very young and wealthy-looking boys had set up camp around several coffee tables, their lanky frames sprawled and draped amongst the furniture. From the theme of their clearly audible jokes they were obviously some way through celebrating somebody's stag night. Alice, as the only lady in the room, could not help feeling rather conspicuous.

'We couldn't find a room that was a little less crowded, could we?' she ventured. 'I feel as though this lot are giving me the most frightful dirty looks.' She rolled her eyes in the direction of the cigar smoke and ribald jokes.

'Of course, of course,' he said reassuringly. 'I didn't think . . . how careless of me, I'm sorry. Shall we take our drinks?'

'Rather.' She grabbed her glass of port protectively. Its smooth, syrupy texture and rich, woody sweetness seemed to be quite the most delicious mixture she had ever tasted. It matched her mood, setting her heart aglow with confidence and pleasure.

She followed him out of the lounge and back into the lobby. There she had to wait a few minutes while he spoke to the rather dashing porter, glamorously attired in red and black tails with shiny patent shoes and spotless white kid gloves. Alice stood in the background, twirling the stem of her port glass and pretending to study a framed print of Lambeth Bridge. Taking her by the hand, Horatio then led her down a magnificent oak-panelled corridor. Dimly lit beneath rows of winking chandeliers, smiling portraits of benevolent old gentlemen seemed to stare approvingly at her as she passed, her feet gliding over the yards and yards of rich, deep carpet. After what seemed like hours, they stopped outside one of the huge oak doors. Horatio deftly produced some keys, unlocked the door and gently pushed her inside. Alice found herself in the most palatial bedroom she had ever seen. Great sweeps of cream silk hung round a gigantic four-poster bed; miles of blue velvet and gold brocade covered the chairs and sofa, which were elegantly positioned between several little glass-topped coffee tables.

'But this is beautiful,' she gasped.

'Yes, I'm very fond of this room too,' he said, switching on one of the marble lamps and turning off the main light.

44

The soft silks and velvets shimmered even more beautifully in the half-glow.

'I believe that pleasure should always be sought amidst the appropriate surroundings, don't you?' He moved towards her as he spoke, looking directly into her face, his eyes and voice for the first time revealing the sexuality that had always been implicit.

Alice nearly panicked. The shock of realizing that it was not just a game, that the entire evening – with her unashamed help – had always been moving inevitably, irrevocably towards this moment and this huge bed, now just a few feet behind her, made her suddenly feel dangerously sober. She wanted time to think, to double-check that this really had been what she wanted. But Horatio, with a smile that set her heart fluttering in a way she had never before experienced, took her glass of port from her hand and set it down – all without taking his eyes off her face.

'And now, my fair Lady Hamilton, I am going to disrobe you,' he murmured, pushing her coat back over her shoulders and starting to kiss her.

· 7 ·

Waking Up

Perhaps if Alice had had a lover or two before Peter, she might have been better equipped to cope with the glib well-practised advances of Douglas Havant that Thursday evening. As it was, she not only failed to recognize the moves in the game as he made them, but she played her own part so well that Douglas was completely fooled. Being intimately acquainted with the seamier businesses conducted behind the jostling curtains and dim red lightbulbs visible in many of the Shepherd Market flats, he had not thought twice about the motives of an over-made-up, middle-aged lady sitting down to eat on her own in one of the most well-known of the 'pick-up' sites. Even if, left to his own devices, he might have given her the benefit of the doubt, Pablo – his old friend and ally in such matters – had given him the nod. Nothing in Alice's behaviour had contradicted this first impression. True, she seemed 'softer' than most, but also extremely adept at playing the old game of building up a bit of tension and excitement. That was how Douglas liked it best. All the ingredients of a genuine chase – initial coyness, a bit of flirtation and plenty of gallantry on his part – but with the gratifying knowledge that they both knew exactly where it was leading.

It was because of this, that Douglas turned to Alice a few minutes after they had made love, and enquired unromantically:

'How much do you normally charge?'

Alice was in another world. Her head throbbed uncomfortably from the combination and quantity of drink that she had consumed, but at the same time she felt marvellous. The 'mystery of sex' – which for her had always meant the mystery of what on earth everyone got so excited about – had been revealed. Feeling ecstatic, relaxed, desirable, satiated, womanly, and another dozen adjectives that flitted through her mind in an attempt to describe this new and wonderful feeling, she did not even register that her lover had spoken. She was trying to think of what she could say to him – that wouldn't sound corny or stupid – in order to express just a small fraction of her happiness.

Clearing his throat rather loudly in case she had dozed off – he wasn't very keen for her to stay the whole night – Douglas tried again:

'Would you mind if we settled up now?'

'Settled up what?' said Alice dreamily.

'The money, of course – how much do I owe you?' He reached for his trousers to look for some cash.

Alice still did not realize what he was talking about.

'You don't owe me anything. . .' she started, now sounding a little puzzled, but Douglas interrupted her.

'I'm not having any of that. It was my choice to pay for the meal and bring you here – that's just how I like to do things. It certainly doesn't mean that you should feel obliged to charge me less than your usual rate. Believe me, I can afford it.' He began pulling five pound notes out of his wallet.

'My usual rate?' whispered Alice, a small part of her still fighting the realization of what his words meant.

'Yes, how much is it?' he said, a little impatiently now. 'Most people. . .' but something made him stop counting his money and look up; something to do with the corpselike stillness that had descended upon his bed-mate. Alice, very pale and looking now much older than her fifty-one years, was staring at him, terrified. Thinking that she

47

couldn't be feeling very well, he reached out to touch her arm and ask her if she was all right.

'Don't touch me!' she shrieked, pulling the covers up to her neck with such a jerk, that all Douglas's money fluttered to the floor. She felt winded from shock and indignation. Her words came out in strange little gasps.

'How . . . much . . . do . . . you . . . think . . . I was worth?' she managed at last.

Douglas, reading this reaction as a pleading for a little flattery and reassurance, blundered on – although she did strike him as looking suddenly very odd indeed.

'Oh at least £80 – I mean I really enjoyed. . .'

'You stupid, stupid, loathsome man,' she said in a strangled voice, 'haven't you realized that I am not a whore.' She almost spat the words at him. 'I am not a bloody whore. I am not a bloody whore.' She was sobbing now, the initial shock and outrage having given way to a desperate misery.

It was Douglas's turn to look incredulous. His obtuseness was not due entirely to stupidity. As an egoist of monumental proportions – a fact of which Douglas himself liked to boast – he tended to regard life purely in the light of his own desires and satisfactions. He had been absolutely convinced that Alice had been looking for a client and had interpreted every one of her words and actions as reinforcing this belief. Letting him pay for the meal, proposing that they go on for a nightcap, agreeing that names weren't important, and then being obviously impatient to get to the bedroom had all been read by him as the not unexpected behaviour of an intelligent pro who knows she's landed a good client and wants to get the most out of him before keeping her side of the bargain. His only reservation had been her age. But he had felt distinctly in the mood for some fun, and knew – from several past encouters – that the more experienced ones were often the best. The notion that he had been mistaken in every respect was quite devastating. It made him feel

48

very silly and Douglas Havant wasn't accustomed to feeling silly.

'Well, of course I am most dreadfully sorry,' he said awkwardly, directing his words to Alice's heaving shoulders. 'But I do think I could be forgiven for making such a mistake . . . I mean there aren't many ladies who get all painted up to dine alone in that place unless. . .'

'Don't say any more. Just don't say another single word.' Alice was still crying, but slightly more calmly. Without looking at him she got out of bed and started getting dressed.

Douglas toyed with the idea of trying to make amends. He could apologize profusely, swear that in fact the whole evening had meant an awful lot to him and express immense delight at this discovery that she had spent time with him for pleasure rather than business. But his remorse, he decided, did not stretch that far. It did not stretch, that is, to risking the unattractive prospect of getting himself involved in this strange woman's life. He had tried keeping mistresses before and had found it an even more complicated business than attempting to understand his wife. He preferred instead to treat himself to the odd night out, using all the facilities of Shepherd Market and making the most of the discreet services always available at his club. Furthermore, this occasion had proved that the old maxim about older women being more expert did have its exceptions. For all these reasons Douglas Havant decided to take Alice at her word and say nothing.

Having paid a hurried visit to the bathroom to arrange her face and hair as best she could, Alice headed for the door, deliberately not looking at him or any of the tastelessly extravagant furnishings around her.

'Goodbye. . .' he began feebly, but she had already shut the door behind her and was gone.

· 8 ·

Getting Home

The night porter who let Alice out hardly gave her a second look. He was used to such goings on, especially where Douglas Havant was concerned.

Alice's stilettos clacked noisily on the pavements of the dark, empty streets. Keeping time with her footsteps went the words: 'Don't think about it . . . don't think about it . . . don't think about it,' drumming inside her head, marching her onwards.

She managed to get herself back to Green Park, where she had no trouble in hailing a cab.

'Turned nice and mild now,' said the cabbie pleasantly, as they sped off towards north London. Hoping for a relaxed discussion on any subject, to help pass the long hours of his night shift, he shot her an encouraging glance in the mirror.

But Alice had not even heard him. She was too preoccupied with concentrating on how not to panic. The immediate answer was simply to prevent any sort of coherent thought about what had happened from forming in her mind. The amount of will-power required to achieve this made it almost impossible. She could feel the images of and reactions to her experience queueing up to find expression, pushing against the walls of her consciousness till she thought her head would burst. Even letting them in one by one, coping with each one separately would – she knew instinctively – be out of the question. The moment she allowed one idea to form clearly – like, for instance: 'You have made an utter fool of yourself' – the floodgates would be opened; and all the words now whizzing round in her head haphazardly, but relatively harmlessly – ugly words like 'whore', 'degradation', 'dirty', 'wrong', and 'regret' –would follow suit, immediately arranging themselves into a barrage of intelligible and therefore unbearable thoughts.

Instead, she concentrated on thinking up a plausible reason for her arriving back at three am. This aspect of the situation, although terrifying, was the least awesome. Indeed, it was almost relaxing compared to the alternatives. The fact that it was so uncharacteristic of her also made it a little easier. Being so improbable, it meant there was a good chance that even the most far-fetched explanation would be believed. As Alice searched her imagination for a good story, she clung to this hope. By the time the cabbie pulled up outside the little white gates of Quadrant Grove, she had opted for a crash whilst travelling home by taxi. A collision with a small van, she decided, had left her driver – but fortunately not herself – quite badly hurt. She had felt obliged to accompany him to Marylebone Hospital where the process of filling in forms and being checked over had all taken a ridiculous amount of time.

In spite of such a lucid preparation of her defences, Alice's legs were still shaking so badly that trying to tip-toe round the side of the house to the back door – the front one only closed properly if it was given a good bang – proved to be an exercise in physical control well beyond her capabilities. After several earth-shattering thwacks caused by a heel accidentally hitting the ground, she took her shoes off and made her way uncomfortably, but silently, up the narrow gravel path.

Next in the series of disheartening events which had characterized the evening was the discovery that her keys were missing. This came as no surprise to Alice, since she

51

was one of those people who believed in the forces of a rough natural justice. Just as in tennis, deliberately calling a good ball out guaranteed the next shot would be a disaster, so it was only to be expected that her venture into infidelity should be punished by the disappearance of her keys and the consequent trauma of having to wake Peter to get into the house.

Resigning herself to her fate, she reached up to press the back door bell. As she did so, a sweet, merry jangle sounded in her pocket. She could have laughed for joy. Silently swearing to be thankful to God every second for the rest of her life, she quickly unlocked the door.

Once safely inside the warm, familiar kitchen, Alice felt calmer. Everything was so reassuringly the same. Her orderly shelves of herbs and cookery books still occupied the space between the fridge and the stove; the bright teacloth saying 'Home Sweet Home' still hung on its peg behind the door and beside the battered old red telephone lay her shopping list, all ready for the next day's trip to the supermarket. 'Carrots,' she thought suddenly, 'I forgot to put down carrots.' The idea was a wonderful relief. Rummaging through her bag for a pen, she added the word to the bottom of her list. After thinking a little more, she wrote down 'rubbish-bags' as well.

Then there was nothing for it but to start the risky ascent to the landing and pray that Peter had rewarded his late night at the office with several large whiskies. The stairs creaked horribly – they always had done. Feeling about as quiet as a ten-gun salute, and looking as if she was picking her way through a minefield, she finally made it to the top. To her amazement, the bedroom door – now only a few feet ahead of her – remained closed, in spite of her thunderous approach.

Bracing herself, she turned its handle fraction by fraction and eased it open. Not waking Peter had by now become the only thing that mattered. It meant that she could pretend she had got home a little earlier. More importantly, it would allow her a few hours of quiet privacy in which to prepare herself for the inevitable showdown the next morning. Avoiding what she knew to be a particularly squeaky board just inside the door, she took a big careful step into the stuffy darkness of the bedroom. No sound came from Peter's bed and within a few minutes she had triumphantly eased herself between the sheets. They felt deliciously cool and soothing. Closing her eyes, she let her mind drift into a blissful state of heavy blankness. She floated further and further into it, until only the tiniest corner of her thoughts were still conscious. Then quite suddenly, she was cruelly, horribly wide awake again. Something was not as it should be. Something was missing. She lay there, tense and expectant, straining her senses to try and work out why the atmosphere in the room seemed so unnatural.

Not even the faintest rustle came from Peter's bed. She listened hard. She could not even hear his breathing. Her suspicions now roused, she sat up and peered over towards his side of the room, screwing up her eyes in an effort to penetrate the darkness. But all she could make out was the barest outline of the bed itself. Now fully awake, Alice got out of bed and padded over to the window. Slowly, quietly, she pulled back the edge of the curtain so as to let in a little more light. The sky was filled with the greyish tinge that heralds the approach of dawn. It cast a sinister silvery beam into the room, falling in a broad band across the upper part of Peter's bed. As Alice had by now started to suspect, the bed was empty. The smooth pillow and neatly folded covers had quite plainly not seen their usual occupant since early the previous morning, when he had hurried off to work on an empty stomach after making uncharacteristic suggestions about dining out together.

Her first reaction was relief, followed closely by curiosity. It seemed too incredibly lucky to be true. In fact so incredulous was she of her good fortune, that she went back downstairs to double-check for clues as to whether he really had not returned home that evening. It crossed her mind that he might have got home late, panicked at her not being there and rushed out with half the metropolitan police force to comb Green Park and Hampstead Heath with torches and sniffer-dogs. But everything was exactly as she had left it earlier that evening. No brolly, no briefcase, no newspaper – nothing. Besides, it would be very unlike Peter to panic, she mused, happily creaking up the stairs with a mug of hot chocolate in her hand; he did so hate a fuss.

For her part, Alice felt neither worried nor suspicious. Instead, like a child who realizes they have got away with an unforgiveable misdeed, she was exultant. Sitting up in bed, her steaming mug clasped in both hands, she let her mind dwell – with genuine enjoyment – on the possible reasons for her husband's absence. It seemed to lift the burden of her own conscience completely. She rather hoped that he was doing something extremely foolish – with that scatter-brained Denise for instance. But somehow she could not quite imagine it. It had been one of the astounding early revelations of their marriage that Peter was even more sexually inhibited than she was. The idea of him being able to persuade an intelligent young girl – Alice could only guess as to how attractive she might be – to spend the night with him, was ludicrous. Glenda, his officious, prickly secretary, struck her as a marginally more likely candidate. She tried to picture them making love in Peter's office, but again the image simply would not take shape. Glenda, always so spiky, cold and serious, was not a character easily envisaged locked in the arms of her boss. Besides, she thought maliciously, Glenda, as well as being the archetypal old-fashioned, unmarried prude, must be well into her sixties.

It was uncharacteristic of Alice to think so uncharitably. But then every aspect of her behaviour had been un-characteristic over the last twenty four hours. She knew she was being awful, but at the same time she was loving every

54

minute of it. This strange outcome to her astonishing evening gave her a releasing sense of power. It all seemed to stem from having done something outrageously terrible; from having contravened every law of what – in her small world – was deemed respectable, and yet, miraculously, having got away with it. Instead of agonizing over the humiliation of being mistaken for a whore, she began to regard the evening as an act of pure freedom. As the first glints of dawn winked through chinks in the curtains, she finally nestled down to sleep, the hot chocolate weighing comfortingly in her stomach. The vague smell of Horatio's aftershave, still lingering in her hair and on her skin, wafted into her dreams, like a breath of fresh, exotic air from a secret world all her own.

· 9 ·

A New Woman

At seven thirty the phone rang. Alice, who had already had a piece of toast and a strong cup of black coffee, took her time in answering it. It was, of course, Peter.

'Alice, my God, what can I say?'

'I don't know, Peter. What do you want to say?' she replied, seeing no reason why she should try to make him feel any better.

'It all sounds so unbelievable, that's the trouble – but honestly it was working late and then the three of us – that's George, Denise and I – went to George's club for a meal; and by the time we had finished it was so late that it seemed sensible to stay the night there. And, well, of course, we did have quite a lot to drink . . . but it was all harmless, I promise you. I meant to ring you – I really did, but once we got to the club, we went straight into the dining room and then, I suppose with all the drink and everything, it just slipped my mind.'

Having been reassured on the one niggling worry that Peter might have been trying to phone her before she finally made it home, Alice felt light-headed with the strength of her own position. She said nothing however, thereby forcing him to go on, apologizing for what had and – as he kept assuring her – had not happened.

Adopting the most contrite and endearing tone he could manage, he finally drew his verbose defence to a close:

'I realize it must have been a rotten evening for you . . . but do you forgive me?'

Since Peter thought he was being irresistible, he was somewhat put out by Alice's reply:

'By your account there's nothing to forgive. Do you think you'll be home at the normal time tonight?'

'Yes, oh yes – tonight there shouldn't be any problem at all.' He wished he could think of some clever way of winning her round. Although they had never been very good at sharing their feelings or being openly affectionate, they had always been careful to communicate with mutual respect and politeness. Yet now – in spite of more than usually blunted powers of perception due to a monumental hangover – he detected a new, unprecedented note in his wife's voice, which he found extremely disagreeable and rather disturbing. For twenty-six years the machinery of their marriage had run smoothly and independently. The overwhelming sense that it was now breaking down and demanding attention was beginning to frighten him. He seriously felt that he ought to be able to do something about it. But there his analysis of the situation stopped. Feeling as though thousands of little men with metal hammers were banging against both the inside and outside of his skull, the prospect of prolonging the conversation any further was intolerable. Besides, he already had the vague sense that he might have fallen into the trap of protesting too much. So, with a last, pathetically repentant 'well, goodbye then, my dear' – to which Alice had to force herself not to cry out with irritation – he hung up, his mind bleary with self-pity and exhaustion.

Alice in fact believed every word Peter said. She placed the telephone firmly down, to make sure the line was dead, and then left it off the hook. The thought that this new, infuriatingly contrite Peter might call again for a second shot at pacifying her was more than she could bear. A steaming hot, perfumed bath was what she needed. While the taps splashed down into a whirlpool of expanding foam, Alice, for the first time in many years, gave herself a thorough examination in the full-length mirror.

Her body still tingled pleasantly from its revelationary experiences of the night before. There was a dull ache at the base of her spine and the insides of her thighs felt taut and stiff from the unaccustomed exercise. Still standing before her reflection, she stretched indulgently, enjoying the strange mixture of pain and pleasure this gave all those twingeing muscles that she had hardly known she possessed. Turning sideways, she gave a regretful sigh at how saggy her breasts had become; but, as she noted for consolation, they were still attractively full and smooth. It was the first time she had ever given more than a second's thought to such things.

Her face shone back from the glass with a shameless glow of health; evidence that, in spite of the mortifications that had followed, Alice Hatton, for the first time in her life, had attained a few seconds of physical gratification more exquisite than she had ever dreamed possible. It was of those few seconds that she now thought, as she extended both her arms to full stretch above her head and arched her back luxuriously. It was like discovering that a fairy-story, about which one had always been sceptical, was in fact miraculously true. Alice, like all women, had been made aware that she was supposedly capable of – and thoroughly deserved – achieving earth-shattering orgasms. But such a gulf had existed between the nature of her sex life and the possibilities of physical delight that she read about in women's magazines that she had long since given up trying to realize such pleasures herself. Secretly she had even come to believe that the truth about sex – that it was in fact rather uncomfortable and more than a little dull – was a sort of immense, universal social secret. Everybody knew it was all just wishful thinking, but nobody dared to admit it – just in case the person to whom one confessed should choose not to own up himself.

So she could not help marvelling at her discovery. The

memory of it shone like a light out of all the sordid circumstances, eclipsing those other, darker aspects with its radiance.

· 10 ·

Coping with Peter

By the time Peter got home, Alice was not feeling quite so pleased with herself. The day had passed slowly. The weeks stretched ahead relentlessly. She had dawdled over the morning paper, deliberately putting off the decision of what she should do once she reached the tedium of the sports pages. She had sunk to the depths of reading her horoscope for the second time when her eye was caught by a small space-filler: 'Ancient Seer Predicts World's End' it read. The six lines underneath communicated the cheery information that some wizened, highly respected African tribesman, aged 101, had been granted a vision of the world blowing itself to pieces in the year 2016. At least I'll be spared that little catastrophe, she had thought, resuming her study of what the day had in store for Librans.

But a few seconds later her eyes were drawn back to the silly little article about the end of the world. For it had suddenly dawned on her that by 2016 – which had sounded so safely far into the future – she very well might not be dead after all. It was not the idea of being blown to bits that appalled Alice. It was the realization that she probably had more than thirty years of life to live. In fact well over half of what she had lived already; which meant she was only half way through her marriage. If she lived to 101, like the African tribesman, then she was only half way through her life. It was impossibly horrible to imagine. Thirty or more years of just being her and Peter; thirty more years of spinning out the morning reading ridiculous stories in the newspaper; of trying to fill the hours in the day; of being without a genuine urge to do anything. Such a clear, ghastly vision of her situation had not presented itself before. This, too, amazed her – that she had not until now realized the full implications of being an ex-mother, of being alive, but in limbo. When the children started leaving home, she had automatically felt as if life was beginning to wind down. The future had narrowed to a small blur at the back of her mind; a blur that contained nothing in particular, except death. Now she saw that there was all that life to be lived as well.

One of the bonuses of having Robin around, she now realized, was that she had always been too busy to think. There had never been time – or rather, she had never allowed there to be time – for such distressing attacks of concern about the direction of her own life. Her mind, always intuitively selective, had provided a system of self-defence of which Alice had been totally unaware. It never occurred to her that she was deliberately filling her mind with a million tiny, unnecessary thoughts – concerning first all the children, and then Robin – in order to blot out the big, frightening ones that really mattered. Like the fact that she did not love Peter. What little delicacy could she conjure up for lunch to tempt the fussy tastes of her daughter? What colour silk should she choose to make Robin that billowing 'new-romantic shirt' that she was always dropping hints about? What book on the theatre would bring the biggest smile of pleasure to Robin's face? There had always been something enjoyable to occupy her mind and her day.

If Robin had been a child of weaker character, she would have been irrevocably spoilt by such attentions. As it was, having an elder brother and sister had made her grow up quickly, bringing with it an impatience for the independence which she saw them enjoying. She had endured these

61

oppressive maternal attentions for as long as she could, being only too well-aware that, with Kate and Simon gone, she was the most important focus in her mother's life. But in the end, of course, it was this claustrophobic affection which nudged her towards the decision to escape to Birmingham. Another obvious fact which Alice's carefully selective mind had so far protected her from confronting.

To spend a slothful, seemingly endless day contemplating thirty more years of tedium and non-fulfilment is not the recipe for the sweetest of tempers. The sight of Peter's grey but triumphant face peering over a huge bunch of red roses did nothing to lighten Alice's mood. Even the strength of her position as the injured party, coupled with the secret knowledge that she had committed a far greater misdeed, failed to give her any satisfaction.

Peter naturally assumed her moping grumpiness to result from a conviction that he had indulged in some adulterous activity with the nubile Denise. But attempts to reassure her of his innocence so clearly irritated her that he eventually gave up and turned on the television instead. Alice had to wake him to eat dinner – a baked potato and stew, made from a red wine cook-in sauce, which she brought to him on a tray. She appeared to be eating nothing herself. Peter ate guiltily alone, while Alice clattered around the kitchen. He could not help being surprised and even a little pleased at the extraordinary capacity for jealousy which his wife was revealing. That night, once their lights were out, he tried, for the first time in several months, to climb into her bed. It was the first time too, in their entire married life, that Alice pushed him away. 'No,' she said, so firmly that he did not have the heart or courage to persist.

The next evening saw no change in her mood. Shortly after Peter got home, Robin rang. Having exchanged a few pleasantries with his daughter he handed the phone over to

Alice, hoping that the call would cheer her up. If anything, it appeared to have the opposite effect. Robin had rung to give them a new address. After only a few days, she said, it had become clear that the rent and upkeep of the place were well beyond her and Bob's means. They were moving in with 'some friends' (quantity and sex undefined) and she was taking an evening job as a waitress. Robin had sounded depressed and cold. Alice had not known what to say. There had seemed to be an unbridgeable distance between them. Nothing in Robin's new life needed her or involved anything to which she could relate. Their conversation was consequently short and awkward. Having briefly relayed the news to Peter, she went upstairs to bed before he could think of any appropriate response that might console her.

• 11 •

Peter's Response

As Peter sat alone in the sitting room, with the sounds of Alice getting ready for bed creaking above him, he found not just a loneliness, but a nostalgic tenderness creeping over him. Alice's heart had been so easy to win. He remembered now his first sight of her, perched awkwardly on the end of a sofa, next to two people engrossed in a conversation that apparently required constant physical elaboration of its arguments. So demonstrative were the couple and so small the sofa, that it would have been impossible for Alice not to have been aware of their activities. But she was pretending otherwise. With an expression of rapt concentration, she was turning the pages of a magazine with one hand and trying to smoke a cigarette with the other. Her efforts bore all the hallmarks of a non-smoker. The cigarette was wedged unnaturally far down between her fingers and her infrequent, extravagant puffs involved placing the tip right in the middle of two determinedly pouting lips. She blew all the smoke out at once, before it could touch the back of her throat; and the thick grey billows were making her eyes stream. The new, expensive, run-proof mascara she had purchased in her lunch-hour was failing to keep its promises and little rivers of black, City Girl tears were trickling down her cheeks. Beads of sweat, popping through several layers of foundation cream, were forming in relentless armies along her

64

brow and upper lip. She was the picture of discomfort – the more so from the strain of trying not to look it.

The reason Peter had noticed her in the first place was because he too felt left out of the party. Both of them had been invited through having been in the right place at the right time, rather than through knowing the hosts themselves. The cause of the festivities was the departure of some parents – the owners of the house – for a two-week cruise round the Greek Islands. The mode of enjoyment was what one might have expected from a group of apes celebrating their release from twenty years of solitary confinement. Those few not engaged in this frenzy of atavistic activity were surreptitiously eyeing each other up; secretly wondering whether they were, or ever could be bold enough – or drunk enough – to get together and imitate the apparently absorbing pleasures of their more liberated fellows.

So Alice was pretending to read a magazine. It had been the handiest weapon against the dreadful prospect of catching the eye of some gauche, pimply social outcast who wanted to get his sweaty hand inside a bra. It was the fact that any bra would do that she found so particularly insulting. Out of the corner of her eye, she kept watch on the writhing bodies draped around the room, hoping for the release of one of her hosts so that she could politely say goodbye and go. After twenty minutes, when she was on the point of going anyway, her knight in shining armour – in the form of stocky, shy, but friendly Peter Hatton – decided to make his move.

The first thing she saw was Peter's trouser leg. He was wearing pin-stripes and the leg looked very smart.

'What are you reading?' he had asked, very formally, very politely.

Blushing terribly, Alice had revealed the magazine's front cover to be headed 'Management Accounting'.

'Do you know about accountancy, then? How interesting,' he remarked, in a way that sounded mature and self-

assured to Alice, but which was in fact his 'formal' voice –
kept in reserve for those moments when he felt the most
nervous and the least sure of himself.

'No,' – Alice couldn't suppress a shy giggle – 'I don't
know a thing about it, I'm afraid. I just wanted something
to read because . . . because I suppose I'm not in the mood
for a party. In fact I was just going. . .'

'Neither am I – in the mood for a party, I mean,' put in
Peter, with a little more enthusiasm than he felt was
becoming. But at this point Alice, for the first time, dared to
raise her eyes to look at the owner of the smart pin-stripes
and found herself very pleasantly surprised. The only thing
spotty about Peter was his tie – a dashing red and white
neckerchief. His hair was fair and curly – much to Peter's
annoyance – and looked as though it had been brushed
deliberately the wrong way – which of course it had, as a
result of his attempts to tame it. Alice thought it altogether
charming. But, more importantly, his grey eyes were fixed
on her with a look of such earnest kindness that she trusted
him immediately.

Acting far more bravely than he felt, Peter had suggested
that they leave the party and go out to eat somewhere
instead. Alice had never been more thrilled in her life. She
had fought off various sweaty hands and drunken declar-
ations in the past, but she had never been out to dinner
with a man before – let alone one that she liked. And this
young barrister, who had been to Oxford and spoke so
fluently and gently about so many subjects, seemed to her
to be that educated 'man of the world' for whom she had
been waiting. Her mother had always said she would fall in
love when she was feeling most unwanted and least
expecting it and now, after years of feeling exactly that, it
had finally happened. So, by the time Peter placed a
tentative, trembling goodnight kiss on the barest surface of
Alice's lips, she had decided that she was completely in
love.

So convinced was Alice that she had found the man she

should marry that she translated every aspect of Peter's character in a way that suited her. If he arrived late without ringing to forewarn her, she never complained, believing utterly in the justice of the invariable excuse that his work had been too important to leave. If he wanted her to spend her weekend preparing an enormous picnic and then sitting beside him, bored rigid, on the boundary line of a cricket field, she was only too willing to acquiesce. Thinking that such devotion to duty was the outward sign of the inner sensation of being in love, she had done everything he wanted without a murmur of dissent. She never took the thought one step further, to its logical consequence that, if this was how she felt, then Peter – who after several weeks had declared himself to be uncontrollably in love with her – should have been displaying similar tendencies towards self-sacrifice. But when he yet again postponed taking her to the ballet, or when he started sulking if she tried timidly to suggest that they should see a film of her choice for once, she always ended up by giving in. Her submission and his contented smile were so much pleasanter than confrontation – an attitude which had gone on to influence every day of her married life.

But it would be unfair to lay all the blame on Peter Hatton. Having struggled for years to conceal from his swashbuckling friends the unhappy fact that he had not quite 'cracked' womankind, he was delighted at finally stumbling upon such an easy – and very agreeable – conquest. For Peter had always been one of those people who secretly wish they had been born a different sort of person. Although undeniably clever, he longed to have the sure-fingered skill and grace of a cricketer, or the awesome respect commanded by the tank-like captain of rugby. During his school days – and indeed much of his time at Oxford – he often thought that, given the chance, he would trade his brains any day for the sort of social acceptability which automatically comes with being an accomplished sportsman. Peter's answer to this problem had been to hang around on the fringes of the sporting set; to win the odd pat on the back for a good set of tennis and to allow himself to be the butt of jokes during the innumerable after-match drinking sessions. Consequently, Peter, who was actually endowed with a very fine brain, suffered constantly from a hopeless sense of not coming up to scratch. The inevitable effect on his confidence spread, like an invisible, cloying web, to all aspects of his life – except for his studies.

The most drastic effect of all this was his secret belief that there was some 'trick' with women, apparently known and used by all his enviable friends, which he had never discovered – nor ever would. Not surprisingly therefore, the entirely novel feeling of being worshipped, looked up to, deferred to in everything, was one that he found extremely pleasant. And it was this pleasantness that he interpreted as being in love. Certainly his life became extremely enjoyable. Large picnics, hot dinners, lots of cuddling, and an attentive audience – never in his life had he been so spoilt. Alice's devotion fed his confidence – starved as it had been for so many years. Like a wilting flower given water, his ego blossomed; and then bulged to monumental proportions. He started taking himself and his opinions extremely seriously. Nor did he mind that the friends who had liked him because, like them, he was shy and unsure of himself, turned away in disgust. In their place came a new, smarter set of acquaintances who went to lots of parties, smoked cigars and worked in the city. Being a barrister – a career which he had reluctantly selected after considerable parental pressure – turned out to be an occupation that suited both his intellect and his new-found confidence.

In short, Peter Hatton felt that with Alice, the disparate pieces of his life had at long last fallen into place. After several months and countless more tender goodnight kisses, he took her out for the traditional candlelit dinner. Peering over a single red rose that occupied a small crystal vase in the middle of the table, he asked her if she would consent to be his wife.

Alice had not hesitated to accept. Not one aspect of their relationship worried her. She still interpreted his selfishness as a sign of her own failings, and his timidity and lack of experience as a unique form of chivalrous politeness. She had no experience herself by which to judge. Those first prickings of disappointment on her honeymoon night were easily squashed, first in the sheer novelty of being married and secondly in the engrossing activity of bringing up the children. Left to themselves, however, those early seeds of disillusionment had secretly multiplied, growing in some hidden compartment of her mind, biding their time, waiting for the chance to push their way forward into her life.

Because of this easy start, it was only now, at the age of fifty-one, that Alice was beginning to present Peter with any sort of challenge. He certainly found her recent behaviour hurtful – to his pride mainly; but more than anything else he was intrigued. Now that Alice was acting so utterly aloof – quite unlike the sort of steady independence he was used to – he found himself wanting to get closer to her. He had got used to her hair too. In fact he rather liked it – it made her eyes look a very dark blue again. At the back of all these thoughts, it was the fact that this wife – whom he thought he knew so well – was beginning to act unpredictably that he found so challenging. He simply did not know what was coming next and it excited him.

· 12 ·

Alice's Expedition

The next morning Alice brought Peter a cup of tea in bed and then cooked him scrambled eggs for breakfast. To show his appreciation, he did not read his paper at the table, cleared away his own plates and remembered to open the window after he had been to the loo.

At the door he gave her a particularly lingering peck on the cheek followed by a look of studied tenderness. She seemed very forlorn, he thought.

Alice had been looking and feeling meek all morning. Not because she was any sadder than usual – in fact she felt secretly rather jolly – but because she was steeling herself to make an announcement.

'I'm probably going out tonight,' she said at last, just as he was turning away, '– with a friend I met at the hairdresser. We're going to the cinema. I expect we'll eat afterwards so I might be a bit late.'

Peter was astonished, but immediately resolved not to appear so.

'What a good idea, darling. What are you going to see?'

'"Falling in Love",' she said promptly, deliberately picking on a film that she knew he would never feel the slightest inclination to see himself.

'Righty ho. Have a good time, then, and er . . . I'll see you when you get back.'

'I'll leave something in the fridge,' she called after him,

reacting, in spite of herself, to the unmistakeable dejection behind his awful, beefy smile.

'Don't worry', he called back cheerily, 'I can fix myself scrambled eggs or something.'

'But you had those this morning. . .' she began, but he was already revving up the car and reversing out of the drive.

Alice was very busy that day. She went to Oxford Street and bought herself a new dress – a blue paisley that set off her eyes – and several expensive pairs of tights. After treating herself to a cottage cheese and watercress salad in Selfridges' cafeteria, she spent an unprecedented £10 on make-up in Boots and then bought two glossy women's magazines on the way home. But she hardly had time to glance through them. It was already four when the taxi deposited her in Quadrant Grove. She just had time to throw a casserole together for Peter, have a bath, get into her new clothes and slip out of the house before he got home.

Once safely out of her street, Alice was not in any particular hurry. In fact she was not very sure what she was going to do. Her body had been operating on automatic pilot all day, acting on impulses that seemed to pop up from nowhere and which matched a mood that she did not begin to understand. Now, suddenly, she felt as if she had woken up from a dream – or, more appropriately she thought – from a fit of sleep-walking. Here she was, dolled-up to the nines, walking down Camden High Street on a Friday evening, having told a whopping fib to her husband and without the least idea of her intentions. It felt marvellous. On a sudden childish impulse, she hopped on to a number 74 bus and managed to get a seat right at the front on the top. A ridiculous nostalgia for shopping sprees with her mother, when they piled on to buses with aching feet and short tempers, came flooding in before she could control it. Ridiculous because she had always hated them and be-

71

cause the one thing her mother stoutly refused to do, in spite of Alice's pleadings, was to clamber up 'that vertical deathtrap only to be asphyxiated by smoke when I get to the top'. She could not help smiling at the memory.

But the luxury of having the seat to herself did not last long. What Alice called a 'yobbo' presently came and sat beside her. He was chewing gum, blowing pink, fat bubbles and smoking at the same time. She was convinced that he was deliberately trying to annoy her. So, as she had done over many incidents in her life, she concentrated very hard on looking as nonchalant and unbothered as possible. The objectionable lad, who was now chewing, blowing, bursting, swallowing, and puffing like a steam-operated bubble gum machine, began to edge closer and closer to her side of the seat, until she could distinctly feel his bony hipbone digging into her.

Why, o why, don't I have the courage to turn round and tell this revolting creature to bugger off, she thought, pretending to he transfixed by the view of passing shop-fronts. Her cowardice did not stem from a fear of a violent response, so much as from all the embarrassment and general unpleasantness of voicing objections to strangers about their behaviour. It was this self-consciousness which ensured that queue-bargers, seat-grabbers, rude waiters, and intimidating youths invariably got away with it, if they were lucky enough to pick on Alice as their target. While inwardly she would be raging at her ineptitude, daring herself to make a fuss this time.

She was having one of these silent battles when the bus conductor appeared and told the chugging bubble gum machine to move to the back of the bus if he wanted to smoke. Alice shot him a smile of gratitude, which was acknowledged with a surly nod.

Her spirits were by now somewhat dampened. This was not just because of the spotty youth and the dour bus conductor. Far more depressing was the fact that she was pretty sure she had seen Peter, edging home in the solid line of commuter traffic on the other side of the road. She could not be absolutely certain of course, but it had been the same car. She was too high up for the driver's face to be visible, but she had seen his hands, which he kept lifting off the steering wheel and slamming down again, as if he was impatient to get home. It crossed her mind that, perhaps still fuelled by contrition, he was hoping to surprise her by getting back a little earlier than usual. Whether fantasy or fact, the thought depressed her. It made her unsure as to whether she was giving herself a treat, or simply sitting alone on the top of a bus going in the opposite direction from home.

But Alice was determined to at least try and enjoy herself. A nice wander round Covent Garden would be just the thing she decided; a browse round the late-night shops and perhaps a coffee and a sandwich. This meant getting off at Hyde Park Corner to catch a number 9 – something she was more than happy to do just to escape from the yellow-haired boy with the bubble gum. But as she got up from her seat, so did he. Mere coincidence, she told herself, as she waited impatiently – keeping her back to him – for the right bus to appear. But when at last it did, and she clambered gratefully aboard, so did the nasty boy. This time she sat downstairs; but so did he – directly behind her. Then he started blowing noisy bubbles right in her ear. The loud clacks as they burst made her jump. Apart from being a little scared by the aggravation, she was sure that a fall-out of pink bubble gum must be coating the back of her hair. No one seemed to notice her predicament or to care about it if they did. Soon she was desperate to get away. Without looking to see how far the bus had got along Piccadilly, she briskly got up and stepped off at the next red light, praying that the boy would not follow. As the bus moved on and no one else jumped off, she let out a sigh of relief and looked round to see where she had landed.

73

· 13 ·

Being Bold

Alice saw that, quite by chance, she had got off the bus just opposite Green Park tube station. Or perhaps chance had nothing to do with it. Perhaps the whole thing had been a set-up from the start: a plot by her sub-conscious mind against herself. Whatever it was, the panic and depression that had forced her off the bus were perfectly timed so as to leave her at almost exactly the same spot where she had so recently waited in vain for Peter to take her to dinner. And Alice, on recognizing where she was, found it the most normal thing in the world to retrace the steps she had taken that night when, as she remembered it now, she had felt extremely happy.

It was getting dark and the strings of multi-coloured lights outside the pubs and bistros of Shepherd Market looked cosy and welcoming. She set about trying to find the place where she had had dinner – not with any fixed intention of going in, but just for something to do, for some purpose to her walking. She even knew, thanks to a matchbox that had found its way into her handbag, that the restaurant she was looking for was called *San Miguel*. But she got confused by the numerous little alleyways, lost her bearings and then, quite suddenly, found herself outside the door of Horatio's club. Without pausing for a moment, she went in.

The wrinkled red penguin-like figure at the desk wanted

to know if he could be of any help to madam, whom he thought was looking rather lost. Alice took a deep breath and said that, yes, if he could tell her whether Horatio. . . But there she faltered, because, as she only then realized, she did not know his proper name.

'Horatio, madam? I'm afraid we do not have a member by that name. I'm quite certain of that. I know all the names of all our members you see. Are you sure you have the right club, madam? It couldn't perhaps be Langhams Club you were wanting, by any chance? The names are so similar – Langtons and Langhams you see – and it is only the other side of the. . .'

'No,' Alice burst in, with renewed inspiration. 'No, you see I promised to leave a message at this desk for someone called Horatio, to be collected by a friend of his who's a member of the club – he comes here all the time – but whose name I simply can't remember.'

The wrinkled red porter was not at all happy with the situation. He was not used to dealing with hysterical women. He knew that his proper duty should have been to order her firmly off the premises since, officially, women were only allowed to enter the club in the company of a member. But he was touched by how distraught and confused the lady appeared. And after all, he thought, what harm could a message do?

So he found her a pen and some paper and tactfully busied himself with something else while she wrote her message. Folding the piece of paper carefully in two, she asked him politely if he might provide her with an envelope as well. Astonishingly, it seemed that this was one thing the worthy establishment could not supply. Before Alice's courage had time to fail her, the little man had gently but firmly taken the note out of her hands and slipped it into his pocket, assuring madam that she could trust him completely, and enquiring whether perhaps madam could describe the gentleman member whose name she couldn't recall so that he could be sure it got delivered into the right hands.

A very sensible suggestion in the circumstances. But it made Alice more embarrassed than ever. She felt sure that the crinkly little man knew everything and that his polite, polished surface hid a deep well of contempt. For an awful moment the face of the stranger with whom she had had dinner and in whose arms she had spent most of that night – centuries ago – remained a complete blank.

'Let me see. He's sort of distinguished looking, between say forty-five and fifty, with a beard. And he's very tall and slim. Oh yes, and he's dark haired. And very sun-tanned. Will that do?' She looked pleadingly at the man.

'Now that must be Edward Graves if I'm not mistaken, madam. Does that name ring a bell with you?'

'Oh yes, yes, now you say it; yes, of course, that was his name. I can't think how I ever forgot it. Well if you could see that this note gets to him I should be so grateful.' Alice managed one of her beaming smiles and hurried out of the building before she could change her mind.

· 14 ·

The Muddle

Eric Wiggins, the head porter of Langtons Club, may not have been the most astute man in the world, but he was certainly honest. The idea of reading the strange lady's note barely crossed his mind. He kept feeling for it in his pocket, enjoying the sense of importance that its presence gave him. But that was harmless enough. He even let his imagination savour the possible implications of how and why Mr Graves might be connected with the distraught lady and their mutual friend Horatio. Several club members were often to be seen entertaining various female acquaintances in and around the premises, but Mr Graves, never.

But the little piece of paper remained securely folded in his pocket. Nor did he mention its presence to any of his colleagues. Trust was the mainstay of his job. Trust on the part of the club members that, however painted the face of a female companion, however uncertain their brandy-clogged footsteps, they could rely on the club staff to show the utmost discretion. To betray such trust would not only jeopardize a job he had loved for the last thirty years, it would also destroy his own self respect.

So when Edward Graves stepped inside the building an hour later, the note, folded exactly as it had been by Alice, was put discreetly into his hand.

'A lady asked me to give this to you for a friend of yours called Horatio, Sir. She was most insistent that I should deliver it to you personally,' said Wiggins, moving deftly back behind the counter and immediately absorbing himself in an apparently vital study of the visitors' book.

Edward Graves was extremely surprised. But the same tradition of discretion that governed the actions of Mr Wiggins prevented him from making an open display of astonishment. So, murmuring his thanks, he slipped the piece of paper into his jacket pocket and went through to the lounge, where his customary brandy and a copy of *The Spectator* were awaiting him. Only once he had taken a couple of sips, lit a cigarette and studied the opening sardonic round-up of the week's news, did he pull out the little note and examine its contents.

Reading it only made him more baffled than ever. He knew of no Horatio – either in or out of the club – and could not for the life of him recall ever having met a woman by the name of Alice Hamilton – for so it was that Alice had signed herself, putting the Hamilton in brackets as a way of reminding him who she was. The note itself was a short but impassioned plea for Horatio to meet her at the Bistro San Miguel as soon as he possibly could, because she felt very much in need of someone to talk to. His instinctive reaction was to ignore it completely. But this proved impossible. The desperate tone of the message was too striking and merely stuffing it back inside his pocket did no good at all. It disturbed his reading, edging its way into his mind so that the words on the page passed by unregistered. It was clearly some frightful muddle and Edward Graves did not like muddles. Something had to be done. The only feasible solution seemed to be to go to the bistro himself and explain to this Alice Hamilton that there had been an unfortunate case of mistaken identity.

The lady in question was not difficult to spot. The place was half empty. Only one woman sat alone at a table and she turned abruptly the moment the door opened. Not recognizing Edward, she quickly returned her attention to what

78

looked like a gin and tonic and began despondently stirring the ice-cubes with her finger. She looked much older than he had been expecting, and very miserable.

Not at all sure how to start, he motioned away the waiter who was fluttering napkins at him and marched boldly up to where Alice was sitting. But since she did not even look up, he was forced to give a polite little cough and launch straight in:

'Excuse me, but are you Alice Hamilton by any chance?'

Alice nearly jumped out of her skin, both at being spoken to and at hearing the name she had only thought up an hour or so before, coming from a complete stranger.

'Yes . . . I mean no. I mean, I think there's been some sort of mistake.'

'Yes, there certainly has. You see – would you mind if I sat down? Thank you. As I was saying, there has been a small confusion over your letter to, er, Horatio was it? The simple fact is that it was given to me. Which is of course why I am here. Wiggins seemed in no doubt that the note was for me – to pass on to this Horatio – which is decidedly odd, since I don't know any Horatios. In fact I don't think I've ever known a Horatio.' He paused for a second. 'No, not one. Anway, it all seemed such a muddle that I thought I had better come myself to try and sort it out. I thought it might be rather urgent. I say, are you all right?'

Alice, looking very pale, was clutching her glass so hard that her nails had gone white. She wanted to ask this well-meaning stranger to go away, but she knew that if she opened her mouth to speak, she would start crying. The sides of her mouth were twitching downwards, and the lump in her throat was so big it hurt. But the tears came anyway, pursuing their determined course down her cheeks and on to the tablecloth.

'Oh dear, oh dear,' said Edward kindly, 'now surely it can't be that bad, whatever it is.'

His attempt at kindness only made her want to cry even more.

'Here look, take this,' he said gently, handing her a large white handkerchief. 'Now have a good blow while I see if I can't unearth a waiter from one of these dark corners and order us a couple of drinks. A gin and tonic, was it?' Alice nodded, her face now completely hidden in her handkerchief, and Edward moved away – ostensibly in search of a waiter, but really to give Alice a little time to collect herself.

By the time he came back, she was much calmer, having got to the stage of feeling more ridiculous than unhappy. Looking at Edward properly for the first time, Alice saw at once how the confusion had arisen. Although he looked nothing like Horatio, he would still have matched her description, since he was a slim man of roughly the same age with a sun-tan and a beard.

'How terrible for you – I'm sorry – such a scene and it was only because . . .'

'Shush now, you don't have to tell me anything,' he interrupted, pushing her gin and tonic towards her. 'Being a dentist, I'm quite used to coping with hysterical people, you know,' he added, in an attempt to lighten the atmosphere and force her to smile.

The waiter who brought them the drinks, on recognizing Alice, marvelled at her ability to attract such distinguished-looking clients.

Meanwhile, Horatio, alias Douglas Havant, ignorant of the drama he was causing in the lives of other people, lay in sun-soaked abandonment on the bobbing deck of a large yacht moored somewhere near Nice. How near he neither knew nor cared. He had other, more pressing matters on his mind. Namely the coordination of his own gin and tonic, and the business of tracing figures of eight around the pert, newly-lifted breasts of a certain Davinia Gorges.

· 15 ·

Alice's Secret

A mixture of curiosity and kindness made Edward buy Alice not just a gin and tonic, but dinner as well. During the meal the low embers of his ego were fanned and fuelled by the gentle but obvious enthusaism she began to show for his company. She seemed so pathetically in need of someone to talk to, to rely on – so unlike his estranged wife Carol – that his compassion was soon truly aroused. He could not remember when he had last felt so needed by a woman. By the time the coffee arrived Alice had given a halting, semi-complete picture of her life and the role played in it by Horatio and Langtons Club – leaving out the fact that she had actually stayed the night with him there – and Edward was holding her hand. The cold, lifelessness of it made him truly sad. He found himself trying harder and harder to be reassuring, to say the right thing and cheer her up. Since Edward was normally extremely quiet and shy when it came to discussing tricky subjects like feelings and how to be happy, this entirely new sensation of counselling fluently – and apparently successfully – pleased him enormously.

Putting his arm round her protectively while they were standing on the pavement waiting for a taxi, seemed only natural. As did the subsequent impulse to stoop and kiss her cheek. But as his beard made the first, brushing contact with her skin, she turned towards him so that instead of cheek, it was lips that he encountered. Lips that felt keen and warm and ready to give love.

Behind all feelings of flattery, novelty and sheer human interest, what drew Edward towards Alice was the relief at finding someone whose problems were greater than his own. Dentistry bored him. The house, for three months now devoid of Carol, bored him. The club bored him. The empty routine of feeding, dressing, working, sleeping alone bored him. He felt more certain each day that his disappearance from the scene would leave not even the faintest ripple on its surface. Living had degenerated into the business of going through the motions. Until, out of the blue, popped up someone whose life seemed even more desolate than his own. So he let himself drift into that desolation to try to fill it. It was a new avenue to explore. Not a fearfully exciting avenue, but an untravelled one at least.

Alice, like him, was on the rebound from life more than from a particular disillusionment. She felt at once that Edward Graves was what she had been waiting for to fill the dreadful, foggy blankness. She did not know that, in his own mind at least, his first advances had been entirely brotherly; that they had been immediately triggered into something more passionate by her own eager response. His lips, when they met, seemed to tingle with just as much yearning as hers.

To start having your first affair after some twenty-six years of marriage is a traumatic business. At least so it seemed to both Alice and Edward. But sharing parallel disruptions in their lives was one of the things that bound them together. There was tenderness too of course; but what they had in common was more a mutual disappointment with life than a devouring passion for each other.

Alice's orderly mind took to organizing clandestine meetings with an ease of which she was almost ashamed. Working out the weekly schedule of seeing Edward came as naturally as making out the list of groceries. And what a pleasure it was to have something to plan for and look forward to again.

As for Peter, he noticed that the settled rhythm which they had enjoyed before Robin left home seemed mysteriously to have returned. He was too scared of disrupting it to investigate. All he knew was that Alice appeared to have become very chummy with some friend from the hairdresser, with whom she had developed a passion for going to the cinema. Even if he had allowed himself to be more curious, he would have been lucky to spot the intricate webs of deception that Alice now quietly began to weave into their lives. Truth had been absent for so long that duplicity came almost naturally. She was both appalled and thrilled by the simplicity of lying to Peter. And as the weeks and months went by she found it got easier and easier. All it required was a little forward planning and the ability to look sincere. The only thing she had to guard against was the impulse to be more than usually attentive: an impulse that went hand in hand with guilt and which she knew would be most likely to arouse his suspicions.

But guilt was not one of her major preoccupations. Not at first, anyway. Edward Graves was her first indulgence in life and she felt as if she deserved it. She relished the secrecy, the privacy of finding an outlet that was all her own.

· 16 ·

Managing Affairs

Edward's wife, Carol, had left him to go and live with her psychiatrist. Disappointment and neurosis at not being able to have children – and Edward had refused to consider adoption – had initially driven her to seek consultation. After finding solace on the couch, she soon progressed to finding even greater comfort in his bed. Edward, who counted Dr Reeves amongst his closer acquaintances, had been totally unsuspecting all along. He had even encouraged Carol to increase her visits from two to three times a week because of the relief it seemed to bring her. When at length she informed him that, after five years of being the psychiatrist's secret lover she had decided to go public, he was amazed and saddened. But the sadness came – as he had the perception to realize – more from the disruption and the loss of face than from heartache.

Being a bachelor again had proved a lonely business. Carol had always organized the dinner parties, booked theatre tickets and made sure that their social life was respectably full. With her departure went many pleasant evenings of her making. Not to mention many friends who either sided with her view of their marriage or who found the new situation too embarrassing to cope with.

The empty house provided the perfect scenario for his and Alice's affair. But they seldom made use of it. Wimbledon was not the most convenient spot for lunchtime meetings. His practice was in Harley Street and Alice could never stay out overnight. The supposed trips to the cinema meant early dinners in ill-lit bistros and furtive hand-holding across the table. The only chance of going to bed together was for an hour or so in the middle of the day.

It was for this reason that the Bensley Hotel in Knightsbridge came to be their favourite haunt. That part of town was always so crowded that Alice – for whom it really mattered – felt safely inconspicuous as she made her way there. If she ever were to meet a friend, there could appear nothing unnatural in treating herself to a little shopping in Harrods or Harvey Nichols. In fact, visiting Harrods food halls on her way to the hotel rapidly established itself as an integral part of the ritual of meeting. It was another way of making the afternoon special: a picnic of expensive delicacies to eat after they had made love. Every week Alice would pop something different into her shopping basket – a few grammes of paté de foie gras, a tin of oysters, game pie, a little carton of some ready-made exotic-looking salad, always with some bread and a bottle of wine. Then she would scurry off to her rendezvous, passing under the beady wet eyes of the fish display, through the multicoloured mountains of fruit and vegetables, the sickly sweet smell of the perfume department, and at last out into the street.

Edward had arranged for the same room to be available to them on Tuesday and Thursday of each week from twelve-thirty until two-thirty. The first time they had met there, he had procured a second key – he refused to tell her how. Grinning at her mischievously, he had simply dropped it into her handbag and put his finger against her lips to stop her saying anything. So all she had to do was make her own way up in the lift and let herself in. She was normally the first to arrive and would make use of the time stowing her purchases in the little mini-bar, checking her make-up looked as though she had hardly bothered with it and giving her teeth and hair a quick brush. When Edward

85

arrived they gave each other a good long hug which usually ended up in fervent kisses and falling back on to the bed. Some thirty minutes later, tousled and relaxed, they would be sitting up in bed with glasses of white wine, cool from the fridge, and tucking into the picnic of goodies spread out on the covers. The first time they had lunched like this Edward had delighted and amazed Alice by proudly producing a stubby penknife to open the bottle of Chablis.

'I thought only little boys carried penknives around with them,' she teased. 'And here, look, I'd specially wrapped up a corkscrew, a tin-opener and a knife in kitchen paper.'

Edward was almost offended. 'It's a marvellous thing, a good penknife. I've carried this one around for as long as I can remember and it's always coming in useful for this and that.'

'I hope you don't pick your patients' teeth with it as well, darling.'

Edward laughed. 'It's just about good enough – look at this.' He pulled out a particularly gruesome-looking hook-type instrument and waved it towards her mouth threateningly.

'So long as it can open potted shrimps I don't mind what else you use it for,' she said, ducking away from the knife. 'But I shall still use my own knife to spread them and the kitchen paper shall be my napkin, so there.' She gave the arm holding the penknife a kiss and offered him the potted shrimps.

'I'm awfully grateful to Mr Wiggins, you know, for arranging that first blind date of ours. I'd rather like to thank him.'

'So am I and so would I,' said Edward, 'but I don't think we'd better, do you?'

There was not one second of reality about those hours spent in the big hotel bed. Which was why they were so easy and enjoyable. It was simply a game. Alice had never played the role of lover, even with her husband, and so at first she was rather shy. But as the months went by she grew to relish this late opportunity to tease, pout, giggle, kiss, and be everything that she had never been before. For the first time in her life she was allowed to be young and frivolous without feeling as if it was wrong. She enjoyed the sex too. Mountains did not move when they held each other close, but it was cosy, comforting and utterly relaxed. Edward was her protector. He had rescued her and brought her to this magic place where nothing mattered except making the two hours pass as pleasurably as possible. More than making love, she enjoyed the feel of her body curved into his as they lay together afterwards, his arms around her, making her feel safe and warm.

On the odd occasion that they did sneak back to the large Georgian house which had been Edward and Carol's home for the last ten years, they had both found it hard to feel so at ease. Carol still had not collected most of her things; and, according to Edward, was showing little enthusiasm for doing so. Presumably the affluent Dr Reeves, known for his success at attracting rich clients, had been quite happy to buy his mistress everything she needed. Edward had stuffed all the most obvious bits and pieces into boxes and stacked them in the hall ready for her to pick up. But Carol had been a hoarder and many of the knick-knacks she had picked up from their countless holidays abroad – she had always insisted they go to a different place each year – still lay scattered about the house. No matter how many Edward relegated to boxes, still more peeped out at him each day.

The problem was not that evidence of Carol made him long for her to return. He simply found it hard to concentrate on a new life and a new woman when constant reminders of the past kept angling for attention. As bad as the Berlin Bear leering at him from a niche in the sitting room were the cigarette burn on the sofa and the enormous soup stain on the dining room carpet. A friend of Edward's – it might even have been Dr Reeves – had made the burn in the sofa just two days after its arrival from Harrods. Carol

87

had only just peeled off the plastic covers – having been persuaded that they could not stay on for ever – and she had cried and sulked for days afterwards. That bit Edward remembered very clearly.

The first time he took Alice home was when Peter had gone up to Oxford for a reunion dinner. The luxury of an entire evening stretched before them and they planned for it with all the excitement and stealth of children preparing for a midnight feast. Edward gallantly insisted that he would cook. Alice was to bring the sweet and some wine.

The adventure – for Alice at least – did not begin well. Peter, pouring himself a precautionary glass of milk before setting off for Oxford, had displayed an unprecedented talent for observing detail.

'What's that in the fridge?'

'What's what?' she replied, coolly, playing for time.

'Why this bloody great strawberry whatsit, of course. It looks delicious. What are we celebrating, and why have you made it when you know I'm going out?'

It must have been the first time in his life, calculated Alice, that Peter had ever noticed anything in the fridge. Simply locating butter or milk was something he approached as a major exploration, doomed to failure.

'Well it's not for us, I'm afraid,' she said glibly, 'it's my contribution to the charity bazaar Martha's organizing tomorrow. There's going to be a raffle for it,' she added as a finishing touch. She had chosen her subject with deliberate care. Nothing was more guaranteed to switch Peter off than the mention of fetes, charities and all related institutions and events.

'Oh, I see,' he said. 'Shame, though – it looks rather good.'

A few minutes later he was safely out of the house and heading for the A40. But the incident left her feeling as ruffled as a cat who has had its fur stroked the wrong way. As she soaped herself in a long, hot bath, she wondered for the first time if Peter had not actually rumbled the whole thing and was just playing games with her.

Edward took ages to answer the door. Alice stood as far into the shadows as she could and felt like a criminal.

'What have you been doing?' she said a little sharply when he finally let her in.

He was perspiring heavily – which was unusual for him – and looked distraught.

'Don't ask. There's a bit of a crisis in the kitchen. No, don't come in. Just go in there and pour yourself a drink – everything's on the sideboard. You look stunning by the way,' he called and hurried off.

'What about this pud and wine, then?' Alice held up her two full hands helplessly.

'I'm coming. Just dump everything in the drawing room, will you?'

Wishing he did not sound quite so fraught, she carefully placed her strawberry tart on the large mahogany coffee table and looked round for the first time at her surroundings. It is always interesting to see the home of someone you know. But what Alice really felt was the niggling curiosity of the mistress about the wife. Not rivalry, she told herself as she cast a critical eye around the room – just plain old curiosity.

Carol evidently had excellent taste. The drawing room was spacious and smart without appearing uncomfortably formal: a polished wood floor, elegantly decorated with skins and rugs, some stylish pieces of antique furniture and a luxurious leather sofa and armchairs. Everything looked, effortlessly, to be exactly where it ought to be. A wall originally dividing two rooms had been knocked down. In its place was a wide archway, foaming with healthy-looking greenery, leading through into the dining room. Even without the lights on, Alice could make out a pair of handsome silver candlesticks gleaming on the table.

Peter would love this, she could not help thinking, surveying it all with irrepressible envy.

'What, haven't you got yourself a drink yet?' Edward's

jolliness sounded rather forced she thought, now feeling decidedly unjolly herself.

'Come on, here's the gin,' he went on, going over to the drinks cabinet. 'Better make it a strong one, I think. The less you notice about the meal the better.' He laughed, for the first time sounding normal.

Alice accepted her gin with a weak smile, designed especially to provoke the question which Edward then dutifully asked. (It being one of the perks of that first rosy flush of a relationship that the couple involved generally indulge each other by noticing and reacting to every tiny alteration in mood. Peter, for example, would not have noticed Alice's deliberately weak smile. Or, more to the point, he would have noticed it but pretended otherwise.)

'Is anything the matter, darling? You look a little sad,' he said, giving her cheek a stroke.

'No, not really.'

'Now come on.' He put his arm round her and led her to the enormous sofa. It was even more comfortable than it looked.

'I just can't help wondering what on earth you see in me when you have been used to a wife with such an obviously fantastic sense of style, glamour and everything.' She waved her hand expansively at the room.

One of the things that Edward liked about Alice was the very fact that she lacked style. She possessed a form of gaucherie – of naivety even – which was a rare characteristic for a woman in her fifties and one that he found rather quaint. It certainly came as a refreshing change from the worldly wisdom of his wife. It made him feel more knowing, more protective and altogether more needed – which he liked very much. Deciding however, that Alice might not appreciate such thoughts, he said instead, with more vehemence than he intended or really felt:

'The trouble with Carol is that she has too much style. It's all style, nothing but bloody style. It's all for appearances. It looks good, but it's not real. This drawing room was like a

90

theatre for her. Dinner parties were like going on stage. She'd dress up, put on a big show that impressed everybody, never fluff her lines and win recognition as one of the best-performing hostesses of the century. I was sick of it. I still am sick of it. If you were like that I certainly wouldn't be treating you to the rare privilege of sampling some of my very own cuisine,' he added, realizing his outburst might have sounded a little too heart-felt.

'Talking of which, I think it's probably ready.' He looked at his watch. 'I reckon fifteen minutes should have done the trick.'

'Can I ask what it should have done the trick for?' Edward's outburst had reassured her. She felt soothed, confident and genuinely hungry.

'Pasta. The only thing I'm worried about is the sauce – it had a sort of solid look to it. Could you bring the wine through? I thought we'd eat in the kitchen as it's cosier.'

Alice had a sudden thought. 'Is it fresh pasta?' she asked as innocently as she could.

'Nothing but the best,' he called back over his shoulder.

Her heart sank. Five minutes boiling was sometimes overdoing it if the pasta was very fresh. Fifteen minutes would be tantamount to murder.

She followed him into the kitchen which looked as though it had been a test-target for a deadly nuclear weapon. Cupboard doors and drawers hung open, half-empty – having apparently ejected their contents at random over every surface available. Even as she took in this vision of chaos, Edward began pulling fiercely at those drawers which had so far escaped molestation, scooping out handfuls of objects and swearing.

'Can't find the bloody ladle-thing. You can't see it can you?' He continued rummaging, his anger and frustration showing in the pink tips of his ears.

Alice took a deep breath and tried to answer in a neutral tone of voice.

'What do you need a ladle for?' she said. But it didn't

91

work. The tone was wrong, mean and accusing. She might just as well have said: 'I've never seen a kitchen in such a state in all my life. No wonder you can't find a ladle – though what in heavens name you need a ladle for when you're cooking pasta, I cannot think.'

He turned to face her, his face shiny and very red. Leaning back against the sink, he folded his arms and said:

'I need a ladle to transfer the sauce from the dish there,' he pointed with his finger to a glutinous-looking brown concoction lying at the bottom of an enormous mixing bowl, 'to that dish there.' Here he indicated a large oval plate, covered with enough steaming, disintegrating pasta to feed a family of twenty-four – with room for seconds.

'Wouldn't this do just as well?' She picked up a large serving spoon that she had spotted on top of the fridge.

'Thank you. That is exactly what I was looking for.' He almost snatched the spoon from her hands and began slopping the sauce on top of the pasta, deliberately making it look as unattractive as possible.

'On second thoughts, perhaps we should eat in the dining room, there doesn't seem to be much space in here. Would you mind taking this through? I'll bring the rest of the stuff.'

Alice was furious. How dare he get angry with her, when all she had done was keep thoughtfully quiet about the whole disgusting mess. She marched through into the dining room, plonked the dish down with a significant bang and scraped her chair as much as possible as she pulled it back to sit down.

A few minutes later they were eating. Or trying to. Even a starving family of twenty-four might have had trouble tackling such a meal. Like glue on soggy paper, thought Alice, as she resolutely placed a third spoonful in her mouth.

Edward may have been proud and short-tempered on occasions, but he was not stupid. He could easily see, even through his anger, that he had allowed the situation to become ridiculous. But he could not make his rage dissolve just like that.

'Used to cook a lot before I got married. Bit out of practice, I'm afraid,' he mumbled. 'I should leave it.'

'All right, I will.' If he had been a bit nicer she would have made more show of trying to eat it. But, deciding that he did not deserve such flattery, she pushed her plate to one side and filled up their wine glasses.

'Lovely wine, though,' he said, picking up the bottle to study the label.

'I just go on the price,' she said.

'Shall we try that pud you brought, then? I expect it will be rather more enjoyable than the main course. Where did you put it?'

Alice pointed into the drawing room where her strawberry tart, covered with a piece of tinfoil, still sat on the mahogany coffee table.

'I should have put it in the fridge,' she said.

The strawberry tart did indeed look a little droopy from its stay in the warm room. But it tasted excellent. Edward opened a special bottle of Sauternes to go with it and their spirits lifted.

Neither Edward nor Alice were the type of people who liked confrontations. This might have been partly why they had both allowed their matrimonial unhappiness to reach such extreme states before, in their different ways, reacting to it. It was certainly why this disagreement – their very first – never exploded fully; and why, once the wine and the strawberries had started to work their magic, they did not discuss what had happened. It was by mutual agreement. Neither wanted to jeopardize the renewed harmony.

After dinner they curled up together in the broad arms of the giant sofa, drinking coffee and nibbling at a box of stale After Eights that Edward had fished out from the back of the fridge.

'Thank God Thing will do all the clearing up tomorrow,' he said drowsily.

'Who on earth's Thing?'

'Oh just my name for Mrs Watermann. I've always called her that.' He chuckled. 'Never to her face, of course. She'd give me the sack. She's one of those cleaning ladies who fall into what I call the dragon category. Carol used to keep her in check, but I'm afraid I let her terrorize me completely.' He kicked off his shoes and put his feet on the coffee table as he spoke, as if in deliberate defiance of the fiendish Mrs Watermann.

Alice could not surpress a twinge of annoyance at his bringing up the subject of Carol again. A glass of wine too many had made her feel rather soppy. She wanted some more of that sweet, addictive reassurance which he had been doling out so readily earlier on.

'I sometimes wish I was someone like Carol,' she said wistfully, 'oozing with confidence, able to cope with cleaning ladies and all that sort of thing. Knowing how to throw things together in a room and make it look so fabulously natural and smart. I mean, those bear-skins there, for example. . .'

'They're goat-skins,' cut in Edward.

'Well goat-skins then,' she went on, too wrapped up in her theme to notice the hardening of his jaw-line as he listened. 'The point is, I'd never dare buy such things because no matter how long I spent trying to arrange them, they look wrong. Too organized or too chaotic. I found out at school – that I had absolutely no talent for decoration – because of the way my cubicle looked compared to the one occupied by the Most Popular Girl in the dorm.' She gestured quotation marks as she spoke, spilling a few drops of wine in the process. But Edward seemed not to notice. 'It was the Popular One who always had everyone crowded like sardines onto her bed after lights-out. Her cubicle managed to look like something out of a Laura Ashley catalogue: scarves draped round mirrors, miniature pots of dried flowers, beads hanging on drawer handles, arty posters and postcards above the bed. But no matter what I did, my space looked awful – messy, contrived and just hopeless.'

Edward didn't say anything, so she went on:

'That's why I got interior decorators to do it all for me when we moved to Quadrant Grove. But it still doesn't look great – I don't think they were very good, even though they cost the earth. It certainly doesn't look anything like as good as this. Peter would love it, you know. In fact I thought that to myself earlier, that he would love it. . .'

'Alice, please, just stop it will you. I don't know what has brought on this extraordinary crisis of confidence, but if you sing the praises of my wife's taste in interior design once more I think I shall become very angry.'

His tone of voice was new to Alice. It frightened her and made her sensible.

'I'm sorry, Edward. I really am. I think it's all this wine that has made me witter on so. Shall I clean up the kitchen a bit, or are you sure that the terrible Mrs Watermann can cope?'

So Alice took refuge in domesticity. She was partly right – about the wine being responsible. But it was the house too. Not only because it was part of Edward's experience with Carol; but also because it was a house, a real home, rather than the convenient, impersonal carte-blanche of a hotel room where they could weave whatever fantasies they chose. Back in Wimbledon, Edward was a lonely man who had been deserted by his wife. And Alice was a frightened middle-aged woman who had recently faced up to the fact that she found her husband dull. The role-playing, in which she could be teasing and giggly and he manly and protective, simply collapsed under the pressure of reality.

Shortly afterwards, Edward called for a taxi to take Alice home. Neither of them admitted openly that the evening had been a disaster, although they both knew it. At the door, he said:

'See you on Tuesday at the usual time, then?'

She nodded with what was supposed to be a bright smile – but it looked brave more than anything else. 'Yes, of course. And I'm sorry again for being such an idiot tonight. I don't know what got into me.'

'It doesn't matter, darling. I think that disgusting pasta was to blame actually.'

They both laughed and felt relieved. Then Alice got into the taxi and went home.

Peter, meanwhile, had not enjoyed his gaudy nearly as much as he had been expecting. All sorts of people whom he had presumed long-since dead had materialized from nowhere. Not one of the handful of old colleagues with whom he would have liked to have caught up had attended. Consequently he got even drunker than he might otherwise have done and spent most of the evening talking to an ancient scout who had been hauled back as one of the guests of honour. Since the scout was a stone-deaf, talkative, dogmatic old codger, it had not proved the most balanced or rewarding of conversations. Peter caught the train back to London the next morning nursing one of the worst hangovers of his life. He had just managed to fall asleep, into blissful escape from the sensation that large, blunt metal screws were being drilled into his temples, when a kindly neighbour patted him on the shoulder to say that they had arrived at Paddington station. Gritty eyed and furry mouthed he managed to orientate his steps first towards a chemist and a packet of Disprin and from there to several large black coffees. One hour later, with a slightly clearer head but still with the sensation that all parts of his body were joined together by rusty wire, he walked into his office.

'I'm very hung over this morning, Glenda,' he said, 'please handle me with care.'

Glenda, well-trained and long-serving, duly filled the coffee machine and set about rearranging all the meetings scheduled for the day.

· 17 ·

The Phone-Call

The false hope of a late Indian summer kept London bright and golden well into November. Then, overnight it seemed, the leaves all fell off the trees, the temperature dropped and winter declared itself.

Alice had lost all sense of time. Up until the point when Robin had gone, each day had seemed to go by more quickly than the last. During those last couple of weeks especially, she had felt as if she was being hurtled towards some crisis. Then, with the farewell to her daughter, time had stopped rushing by. Now it ground along like some lumbering beast in pain. Although the few hours spent in the Bensley Hotel disappeared in seconds, they only accounted for a fraction of each long week. Between those hours, time plodded, burdened with worries and fears.

The seasons passed her by unnoticed save for the relative heat or cold. It was either T-shirt or cardigan or jumper weather – spring, summer and autumn had nothing to do with it. So that first real winter's day came as quite a jolt. She drew back the curtains and stared out at the steely grey sky and the spiky silhouettes of the bare, black branches etched against it. So now it's winter, she thought. Robin went eight months ago and I've been unfaithful to her father for nearly that long. Looking back did not make the passage of time seem any the more rapid. In fact it seemed years ago that Robin had gone to

Birmingham and centuries since she had first met Edward.

Altering the central heating clock to match the cold, she noticed how blue the veins of her hands were in contrast to the whiteness of her skin. It will be liver-spots and arthritis soon, she thought.

A few minutes later the urge to call Edward became very strong. She knew herself well enough to recognize that this impulse was related directly to her feeling cold, depressed and about one hundred years old. For this reason she hesitated, hovering near the phone for half an hour or so before giving in. She had started calling him at work rather more frequently in recent weeks. It had begun as an occasional indulgence, initially sparked off by the necessity of cancelling a meeting. Since Edward was always very sweet – if a little formal – she presumed that he did not mind. They never talked about anything very much nor for very long. It was the reassurance of contact which she sought – a reminder that she did lead another, separate life in which she was neither lonely nor unhappy.

'Good morning, Mr Graves' surgery. Can I help you?'

'Good morning. Yes, please. Could I possibly speak to Mr Graves, please. It's a personal call.'

Now familiar with Alice's voice, the receptionist knew only too well that it was a private rather than a business matter. She was fully aware of Mr Graves's matrimonial problems, thoroughly approved of him finding himself a bit of comfort, but utterly against it interfering with surgery-hours.

'I'm afraid Mr Graves is extremely busy this morning. Could I take a message?'

'Oh dear, no, I'm afraid not. I wonder if you would mind just asking him if he has a couple of minutes . . . it is rather important.' Having got as far as making the call, Alice was not going to give in so easily. Besides, she sensed the receptionist's disapproval and therefore did not believe that Edward was actually too busy to talk to her.

Edward was extremely busy. The cold weather seemed

to have induced an outbreak of toothaches amongst all his most important patients. No less than three of the wealthiest and touchiest had already called demanding emergency appointments. The morning's clinic was full; fitting in the extras had meant cancelling lunch with an old friend who had just got back from several months abroad.

'I'm sorry to bother you, Mr Graves,' Miss Jones tiptoed into the room where Edward was manœuvring several gleaming metal implements inside the gaping mouth of a lady with very red lipstick and wide, frightened eyes.

'There's a personal phone-call for you which the caller insists is very important.'

'Who is it, Miss Jones? Can't you see I'm very busy? There now, Mrs Hardy, you can't feel even the tiniest twinge, can you?' he said, in a gentler voice, aimed at making the two green eyes look slightly less terrified.

'I know how busy you are and that's what I told the lady. But she was most insistent that I ask you to speak to her.'

'If it's not a patient it can't be so important that it won't wait. I should close your mouth just a little bit, Mrs Hardy, as we've a little way to go yet and I don't want you suing me for lockjaw.' He smiled reassuringly. The mouth closed a fraction, but the eyes opened even wider in terror.

Returning his attention to the hovering Miss Jones, he said impatiently:

'Please ask whoever it is to leave her number, and say I'll call back as soon as I get a moment. Oh, and could you ask Nurse Foster to bring me the X-rays I took of Mrs Hardy last week.'

Miss Jones scurried out, annoyed that Alice had forced her to irritate her boss. A note of triumph therefore edged into her voice when she got back on the phone:

'As I said, Mr Graves is far too busy to take a personal call.' She emphasized the word personal so that it sounded almost dirty. 'He asked me to note down your number so that he can call you back as soon as he has a spare moment. But I don't expect that will be until well into the afternoon.'

'He's really that busy?' said Alice, still half-disbelieving. 'Well then. I shall just have to try again another day.'

'As I said, madam, if you give me your number, Mr Graves would be only too happy to call you back.'

Alice did not want to leave her telephone number. It seemed so impersonal somehow. Most of all, she did not want to give the gloating Miss Jones the satisfaction of agreeing to do so.

'No, don't worry. Goodbye.' She put the phone down abruptly.

Alice now felt very angry with Edward. She was sure he must have guessed it was her; and therefore took it as an insult that his work should be more pressing than a message that she needed to speak to him urgently. She spent the rest of the day sulking and imagining what she would say when she next saw him – in a mere twenty-four hours time. By the evening she had convinced herself that she had been nearly suicidal with depression before phoning. Peter, when he got home, noticed that his wife seemed rather low. He put it down to the sudden onset of the cold weather and tried to perk her up by complimenting her on dinner – Alice's cooking was always excellent – and by helping to clear the table.

· 18 ·

The Break

Contrary to Alice's belief, Edward did not like her phoning him at work. The first time it had been all right because there had been a sensible reason. But lately she had been doing it two or three times a week, without any reason at all, which he found annoying. The trouble was, he had said at first that he did not mind – to please her and because he never imagined that she would allow it to become such a habit. So now it was difficult to turn round to her and say that it irritated him.

Edward and Alice had got to that dangerous stage where they thought they knew each other very well. On this basis, Edward was convinced that to forbid her to ring him at work would cause a major outburst of hysterics which would probably end with him having to say it was all right after all. But Alice was not as nervously disposed as he imagined. She was certainly up to coping with a gentle explanation as to why he wished to keep their contact restricted to the bi-weekly meetings.

Alice was equally guilty of misreading Edward. Only seeing each other in a situation so far removed from everyday life and for such a relatively short time made all this confusion almost inevitable. Liking the rough impression that they had made on each other to begin with, they both succumbed to the temptation of filling in the gaps more by imagination than by any real penetration of the other's character. Furthermore, each one, in wanting to please the other, often said and did things for that reason alone, to the detriment of honesty. They really hardly knew each other at all.

As things stood, Alice, since she believed what Edward told her, could not see why their short chats between patients – whose treatment he said he found so tedious – could be anything other than a source of pleasure to him. She could not know, as Carol for instance would have known, how important appearances were in Edward's life. How, even though he knew everybody knew Carol had left him, he would have been mortified by the impropriety of anyone mentioning it other than himself. And how the fact that Miss Jones could now reasonably guess that he was seeing another woman and discuss this likelihood with the other secretaries and receptionists in Harley Street, was something that upset him greatly. Nor did she know how much not having a wife disturbed Edward's sense of decorum. She thought the only reason for their relationship being clandestine was because of her marriage. She did not see how important it was for Edward as well. She did not perceive that in spite of his being separated and free, he still treated her exactly as he would a mistress.

A relationship functions very well so long as it is perfectly balanced. The moment one half gets keener or less keen than the other, it becomes uncomfortable. The one who feels less loved begs for more. While the one who feels less love pulls back even further.

Alice and Edward entered the early stages of this unfortunate syndrome on the grey November day following his failure – as Alice saw it – to leave Mrs Hardy's side to attend to her own emotional needs. Not wanting a scene, Edward played the role she demanded of him to perfection. He admitted he had guessed it was her, agreed Miss Jones was impossibly rude, apologized for being so intolerably busy and begged her to forgive him and to forget all about

102

it. Then he thought, for the first time, that perhaps their affair had run its course.

Part of Edward's charm in Alice's eyes was that he was always so cool and controlled. It made those rare moments when he would suddenly let go and really laugh or, for no reason at all, squeeze her so tight she thought her ribs would crack, more thrilling. But now she detected a new reserve in him – as if an area of his mind to which she had once been privy had been shut off from her. Common sense warned her to leave it alone, not to push too hard, to carry on as they always had and to let him work out whatever worries he was keeping bottled up as he thought best. But instinct and impulse refused to let her behave so rationally. Instinct told her something fundamental had turned sour and that she should try to understand why and what it was. While impulse drove her to claw for more and more reassurance and love, even as she could feel his passion cooling at the touch of her own fervour. Consequently Alice thought she loved him more than ever. When in reality it was the idea of him that she loved and the fear of losing that idea that made her emotion so desperate.

In the immediate future it was Christmas of which Alice was most frightened. She had drifted in her turbulent new world for several months without any real interruption from the outside. Her and Peter's lives were now even more parallel than at any other time in their marriage. They hardly even spoke to each other. She could not remember the last time they had made love. None of this seemed to bother Peter in the slightest, she noted with some annoyance. He was more absorbed than ever in writing his book and would appear from the study only for meals and the odd bit of television.

But now it was nearly Christmas and all the children were coming home. Christmas was usually something for which Alice started preparing round about September. She would keep her eyes open for little bits and pieces for Peter's and Robin's stocking; make and freeze the mince pies, make the Christmas pudding, and order one hundred Christmas cards from Save the Children. She seldom used all one hundred, but in her mind it was a small annual concession to helping the poor. It made her feel less guilty about not adopting a Biafran baby and for failing to send Bob Geldof any money for Ethiopia.

This year, for the first time ever, she had not got around to ordering any Christmas cards at all. Since she always signed Peter's name anyway, it was not an omission that caught his attention. Then, one day towards the end of November – by which time there was usually a neat stack of white, crisp envelopes on the desk waiting to be posted – Alice felt so panicky about her negligence that she took the unprecedented step of spending money in the Harrods Christmas Room. After forty minutes of wandering, dazzled and intimidated round the carpeted acres of tinselled extravagance, she succeeded in buying thirty Christmas cards and a couple of trinkets for the tree. The cost was almost equal to her entire budget for family extras. They can all do without stockings this year, she told herself, marvelling at how ridiculously guilty it made her feel to even think such a thing.

The diversion made her late for Edward, who was not in the best of spirits, since he wanted to tell Alice that Carol had moved back in the previous weekend and that they had decided to try again. His heart sank when he saw the white, tense look on her face. He did not mention how late she was.

'Darling, I'm so sorry I'm so horribly late. I've had a ghastly time and wish I hadn't bothered. But I got our favourite lunch to make up for it. Look.' She tipped the contents of one of her Harrods bags onto the bed and went through to the bathroom to wash her hands.

'Bothered with what?' he asked, pouring himself a glass of wine.

'Christmas. Christmas shopping. Everything. I've been wasting money in that monstrous Christmas department that Harrods sets up every year. It really shouldn't be allowed. But I had to do something. It's practically December and I hadn't even bought one solitary card, let alone any presents. It's all your fault, of course.' She took a swig of his wine and kissed him on the nose.

'With you, the idea of a family Christmas just doesn't seem important – it doesn't seem real somehow. This is real.' She threw herself on the bed. 'This room, you, my new life. This is where my heart lives now. Any chance of a glass of that delicious wine?' The taut look had melted from her face. She stretched luxuriously. Edward felt sick.

'Why on earth do you have to start worrying about Christmas now?' he asked, handing her some wine and opening a jar of black olives. 'There's weeks to go yet. A million things could happen between now and Christmas,' he added, in a half-hearted attempt to prepare the ground for his news.

'Because it suddenly came home to me this morning, that if I didn't do anything there wouldn't be any Christmas. I mean, I've got all the children and Peter presuming there will be a Christmas Day. They expect there to be a bit of holly on the door, just because there always is. And for the same reason they expect Christmas cards to be hung over the fireplace, mistletoe above the dining room door, lots of presents, stockings – not to mention the wretched turkey, stuffing, sprouts, bread sauce, mince pies, brandy butter and all the rest of it. They expect it all to be there, because it is always there, because I put it there. Do you see what I mean?,' she turned to Edward, who had fixed a look of rapt concentration on his face while he thought about how to tell her that it was all over.

'I think so,' he said.

'I mean that if I didn't do all that, Christmas simply would not happen. It depends entirely on me for its existence. And that's why I'm dreading it and why I got into a panic this morning and spent a small fortune on nothing.' She was beginning to look morose again.

'It probably won't be nearly as bad as you're expecting – these things never are.' He wondered if he was capable of triggering off a terrible argument that would make finishing the whole business a little easier. But he was too used to being polite and controlled to know how to start such a thing. Besides, he thought, the last thing Alice would do would be to rise to the bait of an open confrontation.

They sat, propped up with pillows, eating their lunch. These days they did not always go straight to bed and quite often did not make love for several meetings in a row. The first time this happened they had talked about it and agreed that the important thing was seeing each other and feeling close. With the smell of Carol – whose passionate performance as the repentant wife had amazed and delighted him – still on his hair and skin, this was one thing for which Edward was profoundly relieved.

'Edward, darling, I've been thinking. What about me just throwing caution to the winds and telling Peter I'm going away and want to be alone over Christmas. Or I could tell him I wanted to spend it with my friend from the hairdresser, that I needed a break – just for a couple of days. Oh God, wouldn't it be wonderful to be able to spend it together somewhere? We could rent a cottage in Wales, or the Lake District – anywhere – and relax utterly.' Her voice was breathless, her eyes shone at him.

'Whoa there. Hang on a minute, darling,' said Edward, terrified. 'You're forgetting my mother. I really couldn't miss my Christmas Day visit – it would be too selfish. In spite of being ancient, she's still pretty lucid – she knows when it's Christmas all right.'

'Of course, darling, how mean of me not to remember. We couldn't possibly go away.' She thought for a second. 'But I am sure I could get round for some time over Christmas – even if it is just for a few hours.'

She had to be stopped.

'Alice, my love, I've been thinking.'

She began to snuggle closer. But then something in his

voice caught her attention. She sat up and looked at him.

'What, Edward? What have you been thinking?'

He had been going to tell her the truth. All Sunday evening, all Monday, all that morning he had been thinking about it – thinking about how best to explain it. It had never crossed his mind that he should behave otherwise. But now, seeing her terror, he said:

'It's hard for me to explain, but I feel that I would like a little time alone – that I need some time to myself, have a good think about everything, you know.'

'No, Edward, I don't know.'

'These last months have gone so quickly. They've been wonderful, darling, and I could go on for ever like this, but I haven't had time to sort my thoughts out properly. And to do that I need a few weeks of not seeing you. It will be hard for me too, but I think it would be good for both of us.'

Alice was now sitting on the edge of the bed with her back to him. He had stopped talking and was waiting for her response. She did not speak for a long time because she was trying to think what she should say; what she could possibly say to make him change his mind, to stop him from leaving her.

'I don't understand, Edward,' she said at last. 'I haven't asked for too much, have I? I haven't swamped you so terribly that you felt trapped. You always said that I left you feeling independent but needed, and that that's what you liked. So why? What has changed? It can't be the phone calls, can it?' She turned round to look at him. 'Is that it? Is it just those silly phone calls?' Her face was full of hope, a desperate hope.

'No, no, Alice, it's not the phone calls.' He was torn between hurting her more and comforting her with lies.

'Darling, it's not so terrible. All I'm saying is that I want a very short time to myself. You must be able to understand that. Just four weeks. It will fly by, you'll see. With all the children coming home and everything you'll be so

107

busy that you'll probably be glad not to have to worry about finding time to see me.' He tried out a small smile.

'Just four weeks? And then back here, back to normal?' She wanted to believe him.

'I'll tell you what,' he said, 'let's agree now that the first Tuesday in January we'll meet here as usual.' Edward had reached the stage where he would have said anything to reassure her. But he meant what he said all the same. I'll just have to tell her then, he thought.

'OK. Give me a hug, then.'

'There, a big hug. A big Christmas hug for my darling. And now I'd better go – the surgery is packed this afternoon. Don't look so sad Alice, I can't bear it.'

'Don't worry, I'm fine. Just hopelessly feeble, that's all.' She managed a smile, but her eyes were full of tears and the lump in her throat felt ready to burst. 'Go on, go to your fillings and ulcers, have a lovely Christmas and I'll see you the first Tuesday in January.' She was dying for him to leave, so that she could cry.

In the street the curiosity and pity of the whole world seemed to be focused on her streaming eyes and blotchy face. The tears, once they started, refused to stop. She could not face taking the bus.

'Everything all right?' asked the cab-driver kindly.

'Yes, fine, thanks. I'm just in a bit of a hurry, if you don't mind.' She gulped hard.

She fought with her grief for the rest of the afternoon, reminding herself of Edward's reassurances, of their next meeting, of his hug. But in her heart she knew that things could never be exactly as they had been. Mixed with her sorrow was anger – anger at herself. Because she never doubted for a second that she was to blame for making things go wrong. She had found something new to live for and somehow succeeded in destroying it.

· 19 ·

Peter's Crisis

By the time Peter got home several hours later, Alice was still barely in control of herself. Although not the most observant of husbands, even he could not fail to notice that his wife's eyes were horribly red and swollen and that the sitting-room wastepaper bin was full of tissues.

It was typical that Alice did not offer any explanation for her appearance and that Peter felt awkward about asking. But he badly wanted to comfort her. In fact, he had been wanting to have a good talk with Alice for several weeks, but had not got round to it because, as tonight, he did not know where or how to start. But seeing her in such an obvious state of misery, he now felt that he could not put it off any longer.

Instead of going into the study with his whisky, he took it into the kitchen where she was preparing dinner. Alice never usually had a drink before the meal and he had long since given up asking her if she wanted one. But tonight he said:

'Would you like a drink? A sherry or something?' He spoke kindly, so that she would know that he had noticed she was unhappy.

Alice was surprised, but grateful. 'Actually, yes, I would. I'll have a Tio Pepe. Thank you Peter.'

They were having pasta. As she was adding cream to the sauce, she thought back to the disastrous night with

109

Edward when he had tried to cook pasta and they had quarrelled. Her eyes filled with tears for the hundredth time that day and she quickly wiped them away with her apron before Peter came back into the room. That's really when it all started to go wrong, she thought. Looking back, she could see that the evening had contained all the seeds of calamity which had eventually ripened into the scene in the Bensley Hotel a few hours before. Her ridiculous envy of Carol; the way she had gone on and on angling for reassurance; Edward's terrible controlled impatience with her. She felt sick at the thought of how stupid she had been. The sauce was threatening to stick to the bottom of the pan. She stirred it vigorously, unaware of Peter standing in the doorway watching her. But it might still be all right, she thought, yes it will be all right. I'll make it all right. She almost said the words out loud.

Peter began to feel guilty at loitering unnoticed in the doorway. When she started muttering to herself, his discomfort became so intense that he actually tiptoed back a few steps and then started walking forward noisily as if he was just coming in.

'Smells delicious – as always. Here's your sherry.'

Alice was so wrapped up in her own thoughts that she did not even thank him.

They ate in silence. She did not finish what was on her plate and Peter had seconds. He was really very full, but wanted to please her. This kindly gesture was, however, wasted on Alice. Not even the heavy silence affected her – so full was her head of thoughts that jumped between despair and hope.

'Alice?' He had to say it twice to get her attention. 'Alice, my dear, there are lots of things I have to try and tell you.'

'Are there?' she said, clearly not intrigued by the idea. He did not say anything else for a while, so she asked him if he wanted fresh fruit salad, cheese, or both.

'I think I'll just have coffee, thank you, dear.' He felt quite helpless.

They went through into the sitting room and Alice turned the television on. A lady in horn-rimmed spectacles and with a large gap between her teeth started telling them they should apply for floor-space in a communal nuclear shelter.

Peter got up, switched the television off and turned to face his wife.

'I have something very important to tell you,' he said.

He's going to tell me he's having an affair, thought Alice. The idea struck her like an inspiration. She marvelled that it had never occurred to her before. It seemed so obvious. So perfect. So there is a sense to it all after all, she thought. She and Peter would separate. She would be able to approach Edward as a free, relaxed equal; instead of as the tense, desperate wife he had been putting up with till now. She almost smiled as she lifted her eyes to meet those of her husband.

'Yes, Peter, what is it?'

From the tenderness in her voice, Peter wondered if she had half-guessed what he was going to say already. He cleared his throat.

'Well, to begin with, I want to apologize about the book.'

'The book?'

'I know it's taken up a hell of a lot of my time and everything – it must have been driving you mad. But it's just about finished now, thank God. So, all I can say is thank you for being so patient – especially over the last six months or so – because you haven't complained once, though God knows what you have been thinking of me. I'm going to have a small whisky. Would you like anything?'

'Is that what you wanted to say to me – all that about the book?'

'No, there's more, much more – but it's rather harder to explain.' He went over to the drinks cupboard.

So Alice asked for a brandy and sat back in the sofa reassured, ready to listen to her husband's confession of infidelity. And then I'll tell him about Edward she thought.

111

Instead, Peter tried, for the first time in many years, to tell his wife that he loved her. Never – not even when he had proposed to her – had he been more confident that he was telling her the truth.

Six months previously, Peter would have written off the idea of growing to love your wife as being a myth designed to comfort young orientals whose matrimonial fate was decided by their parents. But six months ago he could not foresee that he was to undergo an emotional crisis all of his own; the effects of which would alter his entire perspective on his wife and his marriage.

There were any number of factors which could have brought on this crisis: Alice's cocoon-like silence, no sex for months, a late middle-aged panic – Peter was aware of all these things. But knowing the reasons did not help the symptom: an increasing infatuation with the company's young employee, Denise Rutherford. The occasional, heavily contrived day-dream had been superseded by real, vivid attraction.

To begin with, even if Denise came into the room just after one of his indulgent little fantasies, switching his attention to the girl herself had been no problem. She had nothing to do with the person in his dreams who forgot to wear her pants to work and wore see-through blouses.

Then, on one of the evenings that Alice had been going to the cinema with her hairdressing friend, Denise had come into Peter's office just as he was packing up and asked his advice on how to tackle a case. This was nothing new in itself, since all the partners took it in turns to assign her work and were supposed to help her as much as they could. But since it was by then after seven, Peter offered to discuss it with her over a drink. She readily agreed, and they went to the pub round the corner where the whole firm fed and watered itself. There was no ulterior motive either to Peter's offer or to Denise's acceptance.

They talked at some length about the case. When they

had exhausted the subject they each still had half a glass of beer left, so they moved on to more general topics and then persuaded each other to have the 'other half'. Denise talked a lot – mainly about herself. She had long, dark-brown hair which somehow managed to form itself into enticing little ringlets at the ends. These she kept throwing back over her shoulder, making her long, dangly earrings jangle as she did so. Sitting so close, he could see the soft, fair down on her ear lobes. Green flecks danced in the sea-blue of her eyes. Her face was full of dimply smiles and neat pearl-white teeth. Peter, wondering how he had never noticed such delightful details before, was entranced.

If anyone had suggested to Denise Rutherford that she was flirting with one of her bosses, she would have been indignant. As with anyone she met, she wanted Peter to like her. But, more than that, she wanted his approval simply because it could have an important influence on her career. She had discovered at the age of thirteen that being thought pretty invariably helped rather than hindered a situation. People seemed to find it easier to like you if they thought you were attractive. So tossing her long hair, widening her eyes and screwing up her nose when she laughed had long since become habits of which she was hardly aware. Added to that, she found herself very interesting and was therefore not surprised when other people thought so too. She was an intelligent girl, only a little spoiled by the effects of too comfortable an upbring-ing. If she had known that Peter was interested to hear of her travels between school and university not because he was spellbound by her descriptions of Table-Top Mountain, but because he liked the way her lips moved, she would have been horrified.

· 20 ·

Young Love

Peter genuinely believed himself to be in love with Denise Rutherford. Interestingly, this had the immediate effect of taking the smut out of his daydreams. He fantasized about her all the time. But with his new-found emotion these dreams were now of the long-flowing-white-dress-and-hair-billowing-in-the-wind variety. When he closed his eyes, there was Denise, looking like something from a Botticelli catalogue, appearing out of mists, arms out-stretched towards him, beckoning for an embrace.

Perhaps if Denise had not been quite so ready to try and impress Peter, the whole heart-fluttering business might have died as quickly as it had been born. But she knew that her inclination to fly into the office half an hour late and to nurture a filing system so chaotic that no one but herself could find anything they wanted, meant that she had not found instant favour with all the partners. To have Peter on her side could, therefore, only be an asset. He was a great help, too. For she soon discovered that he was more than willing to advise her on any work problem without even a hint that her requiring assistance lowered his opinion of her abilities. Sometimes – but not very often – she abused this willingness by asking things she knew she could and should find out for herself. But she had always been naturally hard-working – once she got going – and being

114

both clever and ambitious, it went against the grain to make a habit of such laziness.

For Peter, Denise's intelligence was his cover. It was not that unusual for senior barristers to have young protégées – although it was more normal for them to be male. But Peter was careful to speak only of Denise's intellect – always in a gruff, businesslike way – so that his colleagues hardly even entertained the idea that old Hatton was nursing an obsession of a more emotional kind. He was so open about wanting to help the girl develop her abilities, and about seeing that she got due recognition for her input, that it was hard to be suspicious. 'For the good of the future of the firm – too many of our young people get enticed away after we have trained them,' was one of his favourite lines. So even if some secretly wondered whether the young lady's greeny-blue eyes intrigued their partner more than her brains, it never entered their heads that it was a real, full-blown case of unrequited love that they were witnessing.

But not completely unrequited. About once a week – although he tried to limit himself to once every two weeks – Peter managed to find a pretext for a sandwich or a drink with his heart's desire. Denise never once refused him. And on several occasions he even overheard her putting off a friend with whom she had planned something, so that she could accept his invitation. Her cubby-hole of an office was only two doors from his and she made no attempt to keep her voice down. The first time Peter wondered if the person she was fibbing to – she said she had to stay and work late – was male or female. But it was impossible to tell. The second time he wondered if she was deliberately speaking loudly so that he could hear; so that, as he half hoped, he would realize that she did care more for him than for her other friends. The third time he was convinced both that the friend was male and that he was supposed to hear what she said.

In the mornings Peter began, surreptitiously, to take several seconds longer over choosing what tie and shirt to wear. To make it less obvious he would lie in bed thinking about it before getting up. He started locking the bathroom door – as quietly as possible – so that he could arrange his appearance without the threat of interruption. His face was all right, he decided. Quite a few laugh-lines round the eyes – but they weren't so terrible. Otherwise he still maintained an almost boyish look, helped by a round head and a slightly crooked grin. He tried the grin out frequently now, just to make sure it was still there. Apart from that it was really only lack of hair and a swelling midriff that gave the game away. By bagging his shirt a little over the top of his trousers and by carefully combing his hair upwards from a lower parting, both these defects could, however, be camouflaged to his satisfaction.

The question was, what on earth to do about it? Just when the infatuation had got close to exhausting itself, his passion was refuelled by the growing conviction that Denise did feel something for him after all. But, just as one's vision blurs from staring too long at the same object, so Peter's obsession was distorting his perspective. Reason to hope was based on the flimsiest of evidence. For instance, he could hardly contain his jubilation one evening when she commented teasingly that he was looking much trimmer these days.

'Don't tell me, you've become a secret jogger,' she laughed, 'or are you just eating more green vegetables?' She gave his tummy a quick pat.

'Neither,' he assured her, secretly delighted that the painful sacrifice of fewer second helpings of Alice's puddings was finally reaping its rewards. That she had noticed a slight loss of weight was pleasing in itself. But it was the mentioning of it which he took to be the sign of real intimacy. That and, of course, the fact that she touched him.

As the months went by it became easier to have lunch or a drink with her without feeling himself to be the object of

116

scrutiny. His cover story had been successfully bought. It was common knowledge that Peter had decided to take the Rutherford girl under his wing and people were used to seeing them together. Meanwhile, his real feelings seemed to get more and more encouragement. Every time he saw Denise on her own she appeared more open and friendly; and their conversations became increasingly personal. At least Denise's side of them did. She even started talking to him about Billy, her boyfriend for two years. They were in the midst of a trial separation, she said. Peter's heart soared.

'It's just that we met at college where everything was so easy. Do you know what I mean?'

He nodded knowingly.

'So to come from that to living together in London just seemed a bit too pat. I mean, I still feel the same way about him and all that, but I don't feel we've really tested each other. I don't want to be like the rest of them – setting up camp together in the seedy bits of Battersea, trying to carry on exactly as it was at university – lending each other teabags and things. It's so childish, really. Don't you think?'

He smiled, trying to look as worldly-wise as possible, enjoying her energy, her confidence about how she wanted to live.

'I want to give London the chance it deserves – to make the most of everything. And to do that I need to be free.' She looked pensively into her half pint of beer.

'I understand exactly,' said Peter, wishing he could think of an inspired way of capitalizing on this moment of intimacy.

'I wish Billy did,' she sighed. 'I can't explain it exactly, but he somehow seems much younger here than he did at Oxford. There he was head of everything, very sure of himself and so on. But in London he's sort of shrunk. That sounds mean and it's not supposed to. But I think he misses all the running of committees and things he used to do.

117

Now he's just a tiny part of an enormous bank where he doesn't seem to do much more than serve coffee from what I can gather. He hates it really, but won't admit it. Anyway it's made him go all shy and unsure of himself. Funny, but I feel quite the opposite.' She gave him a beaming smile and added: 'You've helped a lot, of course.'

'Don't be ridiculous.' He blushed and felt about twelve years old.

'Oh, but you have. You've helped my confidence enormously – not to mention everyone else's confidence in me, which I suppose is almost more important. Seriously, I really am grateful. In fact I'm so grateful, and somebody told me it was your birthday not so very long ago, that I decided to buy you a present. Just a silly, stupid little thing as a memento of my profound gratitude.' She slipped into a mock American accent as she spoke, suddenly feeling embarrassed. It had seemed an excellent idea in the shop, but now Peter was looking at such a loss that she was not so sure.

'Well, aren't you going to open it? Now don't get your hopes up or anything, it really is terribly little. Just a memento, like I said.'

Peter tried to hide the tremble in his hands as he slowly tore open the red spotty wrapping paper. Inside were two little parcels in white tissue paper.

'Come on, hurry up, I can't bear the suspense. Are you always like this with presents? You must be hell at Christmas. I rip everything open as soon as I get my hands on it.' She babbled on, while Peter slowly unrolled the tissue paper, wondering all the while how to phrase his thanks to her. It was difficult enough thanking people for presents anyway; but when it was someone with whom you were desperately in love, who happened to be some thirty years younger and to whom you wanted to sound as sincere as possible without looking foolish, the challenge was terrifying.

Two china mice dressed in legal wigs and robes stared up at him from the pile of paper on his lap.

118

'Oh God, aren't they silly. But still quite sweet, and of course so appropriate – I couldn't resist them.'

'They are delightful, Denise. I will treasure them.' His voice sounded tinny and ridiculously insincere, so he stopped talking and smiled at her instead, treating himself to a rare direct look into her eyes. He met with such a warm, responsive expression that he wondered if perhaps the time was right for him to declare himself. But he shied away from the thought the moment it had formed. What could he say? And having said it, what could he expect? Even if she were enthralled by the idea of having an affair with an older, married man – and he had read that some girls liked that sort of thing – he didn't see how or where they could meet. But he wanted her to realize how he felt. Perhaps she would admit to feeling something similar – surely that light in her eyes meant something – and perhaps then, somehow, something would happen. Denise dropped her eyes and he realized with a start that he had been staring at her for much too long. To cover the silence he offered to get her another drink. She refused, saying she had to rush off. But he didn't want her to go just yet.

'I think the mice are lovely. Thank you so much. You've done a lot for me too, you know.'

She looked up in surprise.

'I mean you've helped liven up the old firm. Lots of energy and new ideas. You've helped remind me that I enjoy my work. I was beginning to forget. But explaining things to you . . . you're always so interested, it helps make the subject interesting.' You are the biggest coward I know, Peter Hatton, he told himself.

'Oh, I see.' For the first time she seemed genuinely nonplussed. He thought she looked at him curiously. She's guessed, he thought with a leap of joy. In spite of all my bumbling, she's guessed. Now we'll see, he thought, now at least we'll see. But the next second he had changed his mind.

'I'm really very late. I would like another drink,

honestly,' she smiled at him again, 'but Billy will kill me. Our weekly meeting,' she laughed. 'All frightfully formal. It can't go on, really.' She was standing with her coat on and a huge bulky beige canvas bag slung over her shoulder.

'Aren't you coming?' They usually walked the block together before she headed off to the tube and he made his way to the small company car park. He had never plucked up the courage to offer her a lift.

'I think tonight I'll stay and have another half. I'm in the mood, as they say.' In fact he just wanted to think, to regain full control of himself. Increasingly, whenever he got near her, a schoolboy gawkishness descended, confusing his senses and paralysing all normal faculties of speech and thought. It could not go on. He would have to tell her soon. She obviously felt something, he reassured himself; perhaps not as much as he did, but something. By the time he left the pub, a pint and a whisky-chaser later, he had made a plan. He was due to go to a conference in Bristol the following week. It involved staying two nights away. He would arrange for Denise to go along as a useful learning exercise, a vital part of her training – he plotted the exact phrases in his head – and there he would tell her. He would come straight out with the simple fact that he had, in spite of himself, fallen in love with her. He would be as unemotional as possible. He would ask for nothing. Her reaction would have to dictate his next move. It was a pretty rough outline of a scheme, but it filled him with hope. He felt light-headed at the prospect of it and more excited – and exciting – than he had for years. Above all he felt young. He tucked his shirt in more tightly as he left the pub. His trousers were so loose these days that no camouflage was needed.

· 21 ·

The Lunch

November the fifteenth was Alice and Peter's wedding anniversary and they always went out to dinner to celebrate the occasion. Peter would book a restaurant, the name of which would be kept secret from Alice until they got there. Or at least that was how it had been at first. But for the last ten years Peter had booked exactly the same restaurant, so the secrecy was rather a waste of time. It was a place called *Le Château*, down at the scruffy end of the Kings Road. It had just opened when they first came across it and the food had been delightfully light, fresh and reasonably priced. But, when it became fashionable to frequent the unfashionable areas of London, *Le Château* increased the cost of its food and – less understandably – the length of time for which it was both kept and cooked. Their twenty-fifth wedding anniversary dinner had been painfully tasteless and expensive. Recalling the ten pounds worth of leathery sole swimming in a greasy bath of something claiming to be lemon-butter sauce, Peter decided to opt for something different this year. Since the fifteenth fell on a Sunday, he thought it would make a nice change to go out to lunch instead of dinner. Not having had the opportunity to indulge his passion for oysters in recent months, he chose Dovertons.

Ironically, the Hattons had never been nicer to each other than during the months of their respective infidelities. Both were careful not to overdo things with false enthusiasm, but they gave each other's feelings more thought than they had done for years. Peter, of course, had not been unfaithful in the literal sense that Alice had. But after years of harmless day-dreams – and very occasionally night-time ones – this sharp, painful longing for Denise felt like a sin. Not having an affair with her was due entirely to circumstances and his own cowardice. Wanting the affair so badly was therefore tantamount to infidelity.

So they danced around each other, like boxers with kid gloves on, never actually touching.

'I thought we'd celebrate today by going out to lunch.' He went over to her bed where she lay reading the Sunday newspapers and pecked her on the cheek. 'Happy anniversary, dear.'

'Happy anniversary. Yes, what a good idea. A light breakfast, then.'

'Yes, a light breakfast. Have you finished with this?' He waved the colour magazine in front of her face. And on receiving a preoccupied nod, disappeared into the bathroom with it.

'Should I look smart?' she called out a few minutes later.

' -ish, but nothing too fancy.'

Not feeling much wiser, Alice put on a tartan skirt and creamy shirt. She did not feel in the mood for going out; and felt even less so when she saw the shirt had a small oily-looking mark high up on the right hand side. Once upon a time she would have taken it off immediately. This morning she rummaged around in her jewel box until she found a large paste-diamond brooch which she pinned over the stain. A dab of powder, two strokes of lipstick and she was ready.

'I'm going down to make breakfast,' she said to the bathroom door.

'Righty ho, I'll be there in a tick.'

Estimating that 'a tick' meant at least fifteen minutes, she gathered up the newspapers and made her way downstairs. How ghastly it was to know someone so well and not to love them, she thought.

Dovertons was very crowded. They found themselves at a small, wobbly table squashed up against a curtain that divided one part of the dining room from the other.

'Well I don't need to ask what you're going to have, do I?' said Alice, putting on her glasses and studying the menu.

'No, my dear, you don't. I'll concentrate on the wine instead. Dammit, I've forgotten my glasses.' He held the wine list at arms length and screwed up his eyes. Deliberating over the wine was normally a pleasure and he felt annoyed.

'What is that price beside the Chablis?'

'Fifteen pounds.'

'Hm. And the year?'

'1972.' Alice could not keep the note of irritation out of her voice. Not because he had forgotten his glasses, but because secretly she did not believe Peter knew anything about wine. It was all a big show. Unlike Edward, she thought, as her tummy did a somersault.

'Right, then. I shall have the Dover Sole with a green salad.'

'And I think we'll try the Chablis. Seventy-two was an excellent year.'

It was so much easier to act normally at home. Sitting face to face and having to communicate made them both feel very uncomfortable. They squirmed under each other's scrutiny like insects on glass slides. Looking round at all the other animated couples in their section of the tiny dining room, Alice wondered what on earth they found to say to each other. I bet lots of them are having affairs she thought, as she caught sight of a vivacious, sticky-faced blonde sitting opposite an ancient man with wobbly jowls and a pince-nez.

'You get some very original-looking people here, don't you?'

'Hm,' said Peter, engrossed in his plate of twelve oysters. 'I can never decide if I prefer them with or without a dash of Tabasco.'

'Why don't you try half with and half without? There's some juice rolling down your chin, Peter.'

He wiped it without seeming to notice her distaste. 'But then, which one do I eat last? You have to save the best till last, you see, and I can never decide.'

'That's what comes from being an only child.'

'I beg your pardon?'

'Saving the best till last. That's what they say. That children from large families always gobble up the best bits first – before their brothers and sisters can get to them. But where there's only one child, there's no need.'

'Oh really? I never noticed our lot doing that.'

'No, they didn't. I suppose because I used to cook too much – they always knew there was more. In large, poor families I expect it's true.'

And so the conversation ground on, stiffly, laboriously, like an invalid who has forgotten how to walk.

Alice had finished with her sole long before Peter had got through his oysters. Approaching each one was a major operation in its own right. A sip of wine first; then minutes of hovering over the plate before electing the next in line; more hovering over the Tabasco; then the final agonizing decision as to whether to swallow it whole or succumb to the temptation of a good chew. Alice, knowing the ritual by heart, could hardly bear to watch. Placing her hand palm-downwards on the table next to her wine glass, she sneaked a look at the time. A quarter to two and they hadn't even ordered the dessert. And Peter was bound to want a liqueur with his coffee.

'I don't know if it was the sole, but I really don't feel very well. I think I had better go to the bathroom a second.'

'Oh Alice, I am sorry.' He got up from his chair as if to accompany her.

124

'No, Peter, sit down. I'm all right, honestly. I just feel a little queasy suddenly, that's all.'

After a few minutes she came back to the table and whispered that she had been sick and was going to take a taxi home. 'But I absolutely forbid you to move. If you insist on coming with me, then I won't go. It's bad enough my half-spoiling the occasion, I don't want to ruin it completely by dragging you off as well.'

Peter made a show of protest. But, recognizing the firmness in her voice and feeling the persuasive presence of the two largest oysters still on his plate, he agreed to let her go home alone.

Once outside, Alice took a deep breath of fresh air and looked forward to a long, uninhibited chat to Edward on the telephone.

It was a relief for Peter as well. Looking round to make sure no one was watching, he swopped his empty glass for Alice's full one and then returned his undivided attention to his plate. The delicious prospect of a creamy pudding, coffee, a brandy and perhaps – since Alice wasn't there – a large cigar, settled comfortably at the back of his mind, making the remaining oysters taste even better than the first ten.

As he was waiting for his lemon meringue pie and cream, he became aware for the first time that there were people sitting immediately on the other side of the curtain beside him. They were clearly two females and one of the voices sounded familiar. Because of that – for Peter was not an eavesdropper by nature – he strained his ears to catch what they were saying.

'. . . you poor thing. There's nothing worse than an old lech. Is he really revolting – as revolting as mine?' This with giggles from a squeaky, unfamiliar voice.

'Worse, much worse. Honestly, Samantha, at least Charlie or whatever he's called sounds as though he has a scrap or two of charm. He doesn't sound nearly so persistent – or as repulsive for that matter – as mine.'

The waiter then arrived and they broke off their conversation to order. It was at that point that Peter realized to whom the familiar voice belonged. It had sounded too low at first – because of the higher octaves used by the friend. But there was no mistaking the fact the person sitting some three or four inches away from him on the other side of the curtain was Denise Rutherford. His palms felt damp. Using his napkin, he dabbed at the beads of sweat which he could feel, like thousands of minute pin-pricks, appearing on his forehead. He was delighted and petrified.

'Cheers. Here's to the good old days.' There was an accompanying chink of glasses.

'Well hardly, but cheers anyway. It's good to see you,' said Denise.

'Go on then, describe him – right down to the last wart,' persisted her friend.

'Who, for goodness sake?'

'Your lech, silly. I'm intrigued. I've decided to do a survey on the characteristics of old lechers. At least it would be a hell of a sight more interesting than the housewife's deepest fears about her loo-cleaner. Oh go on, Denise, cheer me up.'

'He's a classic case. Going bald, big belly, watery eyes and horrid drooly lips which he licks whenever he sees me coming.'

Samantha shrieked with laughter.

'Samantha, shut up, for goodness sake,' said Denise, obviously trying not to laugh herself, 'they'll throw us out and I'm starving. Are you sure you can wangle this on to your expense account – because I really haven't got a bean.'

'Yes, everybody does it. And anyway it's my lech who signs all my expense chits, so he's hardly going to refuse, is he?'

'Seriously though,' said Denise, 'doesn't it disgust and depress you? All these old codgers, bored with their own fat, blue-rinse wives, feeling they can take advantage of their positions to have a good ogle and use you as fuel for a few wet dreams.'

'If it was just an ogle I wouldn't mind,' said Samantha. 'The most annoying thing is the way Charlie uses his age as a sort of shield for what he's really getting up to. By playing the old grandpa he gets to lay his hairy paws on me – or tries to – while onlookers think it's just a harmless old man enjoying the spirit of youth, or some such rubbish. He's supposed to be happily married but it's bloody obvious he's not.'

'An old geezer, fed up with his wife and rather lonely, I could almost cope with,' put in Denise. 'I think what is really wrong – and I mean morally wrong – is this business of having to play along with them because of their superior positions and our dependence on them for success.'

Peter's lemon meringue pie clogged in his throat. To begin with the substance of their conversation had not meant anything to him – he had been too busy enjoying his secret proximity to Denise. At the mention of old men going bald, his ears had pricked up – simply because it was a subject on which he felt extremely sensitive, not because he thought of himself as an old man. Then he started listening properly. When Denise mentioned bored old codgers and wet dreams, he thought: the poor girl is being hassled by some horrible old man, how unpleasant for her. It was only when she complained about having to play along, because of the old man's superior position and importance to her, that it dawned on him who this 'old lech' must be.

The waiter was offering him more coffee. Shaking his head, he whispered 'brandy, please' so quietly that the man bent right down near his ear and asked him to repeat it. It was partly shock and partly fear at being discovered. Even Denise, with all her youthful confidence, might feel embarrassed at finding that the object of her character-assassination had been sitting less than one foot away from

127

her. Nor was the execution over. Peter longed to get away, but he was equally thirsty to hear more. Like a wife masochistically curious about the physical details of a newly-discovered mistress, he felt a cruel need to know it all.

'Invitations,' Denise was saying, 'all the time. Drinks, lunches – non-stop. And it is hard to say "no", I don't care what anybody says. It's just a question of accepting, being as polite as possible and not giving them any silly ideas – more than the ones they've got already, that is.'

Peter slumped further into his chair, feeling a real, physical pain in his chest. He wondered if he was going to have a heart attack. The idea seemed attractive. More likely to be heartburn, he thought morosely, feeling that such an indignity would suit Denise's opinion of him only too well. Never in his life had he felt more sorry for himself. There now formed in his mind, like a cold weight, a clear, flat picture of what he had become. Until then he had seen himself only as he felt – nervous, guilty yes, but alive with the thrill of a new focus and the anticipation of fulfilment. In short, he had felt like a man in love – with all the usual hopes and fears of success and rejection that go with such a condition. True, the age-gap had been a worry, but certainly not one that lumped him in the old lech category. Confronting this image hurt him deeply.

He whispered to the waiter for another brandy and a Havana, and then made his way to the gents, weaving slowly between the small tables, shoulders stooping, his head hung low, like an old man.

Staring at his face in the mirror, he saw the bald patch shining obstinately through the thin roof of hair, the broken blood vessels on his nose and cheeks, the watery eyes . . . no wonder she feels as she does, he thought, surrendering utterly to great waves of self-pity and self-loathing. And as he stared, what he had felt for Denise – what he had taken for love – began to dissolve. A psychiatrist might say that this was purely self-defence at

128

the disgusting thing he was frightened of becoming – or that he had already nearly become. For Peter, it was just like an exorcism of one huge lump of emotion; he could almost feel it leave his body. And once it had gone, he felt better – not much, but a little. He washed his hands, splashed his face and returned to his liqueur and cigar. He was trapped in the restaurant by the presence of Denise. He simply could not bear taking the risk of being seen by her.

Fortunately the girls were both trying to lose weight and consequently talked each other out of having a dessert. They had a long discussion about the merits of various diets, during which Samantha seemed to get genuinely depressed. Peter supposed she must be rather plump; unlike Denise, he thought wistfully and then checked himself.

'Overweight, over-worked and over-fed-up. Oh God, Denise, I just can't face the thought of work tomorrow. No doubt Charlie will come up with some intimate little project that he feels the two of us should "work on very closely" ' – she lowered her voice and spoke slowly in what Peter presumed was an imitation of her boss. 'At least your lech is at a safe distance now that you've left Oxford.'

'Not safe enough unfortunately. It doesn't stop him ringing to try – for the umpteenth time – to talk me into going back to do research. Research! Can you imagine? I can't think of anything more tedious. And unlike you, of course, I love my job.'

'Have you still got that "front-line supporter" you were on about? What was he called. . .'

'Hatton, Peter Hatton. I sure have.' There was a moments interruption during which Denise asked for the bill and Peter held his breath. He was sure they must be able to hear the racing thuds of his heart through the curtain.

'Now there's an example of how to be friendly without being lecherous. He's pretty old, but terribly sweet and – well it's just obvious that he's one of the ones that really is

129

happily married. He doesn't have even the whiff of an ulterior motive about him. I was a fraction worried to begin with, because he sort of stares sometimes without saying anything, but I've seen him do it to everybody – including his old bag of a secretary – so it can't be a sign of passion.' She laughed. 'I know he likes me all right – but it really does seem to come from a respect for my abilities, not my body . . . God, Samantha, it's gone three, we're going to miss the film. Flash credit cards are all very well but they take forever.'

'There we are, all done,' said Samantha a few moments later. 'Humphrey Bogart here we come. I remember watching this one at school on one of those interminable Sunday afternoons. We cried and cried, do you remember?'

There was the sound of scraping chairs and the rustling of bags and coats.

'No, that was "For Whom the Bell Tolls", silly. . .' and their voices trailed off out of the restaurant.

Peter felt like a man whose death-sentence has been repealed at the last second. In two hours he had been through more emotional trauma than in his entire life. He felt exhausted and suddenly rather drunk. So it's all right to love her after all, he told himself. He sat back to enjoy the moment. But nothing happened. The infatuation really had gone. Only affection and gratitude flooded into his heart – of the sort one might feel after being pulled back from the edge of a cliff-top.

Once outside the restaurant, he turned up the collar of his overcoat against the chilly wind and set off walking rather than looking for a taxi. What had happened was in a way so bizarre that he wanted time to think about it. Peter was not remotely superstitious or religious; indeed he prided himself in adopting a consistently pragmatic and cynical attitude to life. The world, he thought, was an entirely haphazard system in which getting a smooth or a rough deal depended on a process comparable to the fund-raising draws that Alice occasionally got involved in.

Having realized from an early age that he had pulled out a winning number, this chaos was not something that worried him unduly.

But now he had the distinct impression that the intense two hours in Dovertons had, in some strange way, been meant to happen. Or at least the coincidence of Alice leaving him alone, Denise sitting within hearing range, but out of sight, and the subject of the girls' conversation was so startling that his usual scepticism failed him. He felt humbled by the experience, as if it had taught him something terribly important. By the time he looked up to hail a passing cab, he was already halfway towards realizing what this was.

· 22 ·

Bad Timing

It took a couple more weeks for Peter to come to a full understanding of what this gruelling twenty-sixth anniversary lunch meant to him. Weeks during which he consciously tried to fathom what both he and the rest of the world were feeling. Glenda, his dragon-like secretary, nearly fainted at being given a bunch of flowers and asked if she felt he had been working her too hard; Denise found that she was invited to have drinks less often, but that he seemed more anxious than ever to help her with her work; and his colleagues muttered to each other that old Peter had gone a bit soft. Only Alice failed to register any difference in her husband – and that was because she was so wrapped up in her new life that she hardly noticed his existence.

And it was only Alice whom Peter felt he could get no closer to understanding. He made a conscious effort to hurry up with the book, which he knew had been taking up far too much of his time. Although for him the subject of company law held fascinating avenues for exploration, he was very aware that to Alice it meant nothing at all. She might be pleased – and a little proud – when the thing finally appeared in print, but in the meantime it had been a highly time-consuming process in which she could not have felt remotely involved. So now, between his stints in the study, he made the first genuine attempts in years to get through to her. The only conclusion he was able to draw was that she was depressed, and unwilling, after two decades of silence, to tell him why.

In fact Alice was not especially depressed – at least no more than usual. But, as a guard against any revelation of her other life, she had taken to operating at home in a safe, machine-like way. She did all that she was supposed to do – all that she had always done. So nothing was different on the surface. But since it was all done for form's sake alone, her performance lacked true animation and it was this that the new, doubly sensitive Peter was detecting and mis-interpreting.

Denise's short account of how she felt about Peter Hatton in Dovertons was in many ways a declaration of faith – in his character, his motives and his marriage. At least this was how it touched Peter most. If this young girl, for whom he had a genuine affection, believed in this good person, then it somehow made it more possible for that good person to exist. It was as if he had been presented with a clear choice as to what type of human he wished to be: a pitiable, scheming old devil or an ageing, but kind and happily married man. Horror that he had come so close to being the former, automatically pushed him towards the latter. One result of this – apart from a new generosity of spirit – was that he began to think honestly about his marriage, about Alice and about their isolation from each other. And for the first time it began to bother him. Perhaps the realization that he was getting older made him more anxious to find happiness in what he had. Whatever it was, trying to understand Alice soon became more than just another aspect of his renewed feelings of benevolence towards the world. It became a real challenge, like a second courtship. And in the process he found himself falling in love with her all over again.

If, however, there was a guardian angel watching over the life of Peter Hatton, it could not have got the timing of his emotional conversion more wrong. Not only was Alice

133

sliding steadily further away just as Peter was starting to scrabble after her; but also, on the night that he opted to declare his affections, fear of losing Edward had besieged her heart. She could not have been in a less sympathetic mood for receiving Peter's news.

The stumbling way in which he explained his feelings was in itself proof of his sincerity. When it dawned on Alice that her husband was saying exactly the opposite to what she had been expecting, her first instinct was to stop him. But interrupting would have necessitated saying something herself and her mind had gone numb. She had not the faintest idea how to react. So she focused her eyes on a vase, just to the right of Peter's head, and tried to hide how astonished and embarrassed she was.

Peter was embarrassed as well. He felt as though he were taking his clothes off in front of her for the first time. It was something he wanted to do, but which made him painfully self-conscious.

'I never stopped caring for you, you know,' he went on. 'It was just that for a while I seemed to forget that I did –care for you that is. The children always took up so much of your time and, well . . . we rather got out of the habit of talking, didn't we? And it's hard just to slip back into it again. But I suppose, with Robin gone, I've been noticing it more and realizing that I've actually been feeling lonely – which can't be a good thing for a married chap,' he added, trying to provoke a reaction from the dazed stare that Alice seemed to have fixed somewhere around his right ear-lobe. She didn't say anything, so he went on: 'Alice, my dear, the truth is we've never been very good at talking. It never seemed to matter before. But lately it's struck me that however much of a terrible jumble it is, we've only got this life and we ought to be able to enjoy it – together.' Feeling clumsy, he ploughed on nevertheless, making only one compromise with honesty: he made no reference to Denise or the experience which had proved to be the catalyst for bringing his attitudes and emotions into line. He was feeling brave, but not that brave.

'I suppose, in a way, what I'm trying to say is that we should give it another go. Hell, Alice, we've got another thirty-odd years in us yet!' he said, with a genuine laugh. 'What do you say, old thing, eh?' He came and sat next to her on the sofa and took her hand. He noticed that the palm was damp. 'I know you've not been very happy recently; that it's been hellish for you with an empty house and me locked up in my study all evening. But you've been marvellous, do you know that? You just got on with things, made that new friend from the hairdresser and battled on, without even a word against me.' Tears came to Alice's eyes.

'Don't be sad, my darling heart, don't be sad,' he said, stroking her hair. Alice then started to cry properly, moved by Peter's compassion for her and her own despair.

If only Peter's little crisis with Denise could have taken place several months earlier. Her loneliness immediately after Robin's departure had been so acute that she would have welcomed almost any affection – as indeed she had done in the fleeting embrace of the elusive Horatio. But now it was all too late. It was Edward whom she wanted to hold her hand and stroke her head, not Peter. A fact which made her cry all the more.

But she could not shelter behind the tears for ever. As they started drying up she began to hiccough and Peter rushed off to get her a glass of water, giving her a moment's grace to collect her thoughts.

'Thank you,' she whispered when he returned, 'but I think they've gone already.' She gave a weak smile.

'There's so much to look forward to, you know, Alice.' She looked at him, almost in hope. 'There's Christmas, for a start. The children – won't it be wonderful to see them again? I sometimes think I've forgotten what the rascals look like.' He put his arm round her and pulled her back to sit beside him on the sofa. Not having sat so intimately for

135

years, it felt very strange. To Alice the strangeness meant discomfort. Whereas to Peter it was thrilling. Marvelling at how simple life was if you made it so, he felt more confident and happy by the second.

'And then after Christmas we'll go away. A long break in the sun somewhere. The office owe me months of holiday – and it's about time we treated ourselves. A second honeymoon – how about that?'

Alice knew she had to say something. But everything he said filled her with horror. The idea of all the children – which would once have set her heart soaring – terrified her. They were part of a life and a person that no longer existed. She could not imagine what she would say to them, or how she could kiss them hello, even. As for the suggestion of a second honeymoon, it was almost laughable in view of her real desire to get away with Edward for just such a holiday.

'Peter, I don't know what to say,' she admitted. 'All this feels so . . . well . . . strange, that I'm a little confused, to be honest.'

'Alice, I just want you to be happy – us to be happy. It's never too late to start, it can't be.' He tightened the grip of his arm around her shoulders. He was not altogether surprised that she should appear so shell-shocked by what he'd been saying. He too felt shell-shocked – with delight at the new world of possibilities that he now saw opening before them.

'Don't worry, my darling,' he murmured, kissing the top of her head. 'We won't rush things. It's bound to take a little while to get to know each other again after all this time. You can just relax and stop worrying, everything's going to be all right. I know it.'

I wish it were, thought Alice, I only wish it were.

· 23 ·

Christmas Shopping

During the last couple of weeks before Christmas Peter treated Alice as if she was convalescing from a serious illness. Since their frank talk – for so Peter regarded it – she seemed, if anything, more unhappy and certainly more fragile. It was part of his natural arrogance that he put this down to being some sort of 'delayed reaction' to several months of misery. It never entered his mind either that she would not want his love or that she could not love him. So he showered her with bunches of flowers, surprise presents and dinners at expensive restaurants. He even cooked her supper one evening – a rather grey-looking scrambled egg – which was served with much aplomb, and a bottle of white wine, on their laps in the sitting room. Of course Alice was grateful – and sometimes touched – by all these attentions. But gratitude is no substitute for love. It also made her feel guilty in a way that she never had during the times when they got on with their own lives and ignored each other. Before, loving Edward had been a justly deserved treat in an otherwise empty and unloved existence. Now it wasn't so easily excused.

One advantage of Peter's new-found enthusiasm for family life was that he more or less took over the preparations for Christmas, so relieving Alice of a burden for which she hardly had the heart. Instead of spending his weekends behind the study door, he now happily volunteered to go hunting for a Christmas tree, to put up the decorations and – most remarkable of all – to buy presents for the children. The food – all the mincepies, the cake and truffles that Alice had made so far in advance every other year – they bought together from Harrods on the last Saturday before Christmas. In the food halls Peter was like a child in a toyshop. He was mesmerized by the extravagant displays and the rich array of expensive goodies. They went in planning to buy just a couple of things. They came out – in spite of the crowds which made Alice feel so faint that she kept diving for exit doors like a swimmer coming up for air – with bags bulging full of extra treats: port, stilton, exotic dried fruits, a bumper tin of Quality Street, smoked salmon, caviar, and three bottles of champagne. Alice, wondering if any of the staff recognized the lady who always bought a 'picnic' lunch on Tuesdays and Thursdays, felt more lonely than ever.

The only omission in the run-up to Christmas was the Christmas cards. Peter automatically presumed Alice had done them weeks ago and she did not dare to disillusion him. It did not seem to affect the stack wedged into their letter-box each morning. I suppose that will happen next year, she thought, but without managing to feel very worried about it.

When they came back from Harrods, they were struggling with all the bags at the front door when the phone started ringing. Alice, fired with the sudden premonition that it was Edward, dropped her shopping, grabbed the keys from Peter's fumbling hands and was inside in seconds. As she picked up the receiver it went dead.

'With that sort of speed you deserved to get there,' he said good-humouredly.

'I just had the feeling it was important, I don't know why,' she said, feeling ridiculously disappointed. At that second the ringing began again. Although she started towards it, Peter was nearer and got there first. Alice immediately busied herself with the kettle, wondering what Edward would say when he heard Peter's voice.

'Turn that bloody tap off can you, Alice, I can't hear a thing . . . Hello. . . Hello. . . Yes, yes of course.' He put his hand over the receiver. 'It's America, it must be Simon.' Alice's heart had the audacity to sink. But she went to Peter's side to try and hear the conversation.

'Hello? Simon? Yes it's Dad. How are you?. . . What? Yes, yes, terrible line. . . Yes, yes we're fine . . . We got your postcard – what time are you arriving?' Then there was a long silence while Peter listened to his son and Alice strained, unsuccessfully, to catch what was being said.

'Oh,' he said at last, 'oh I see. Well that sounds terrific. . . No, no of course not . . . and after that? . . . I see, yes, how wonderful . . . and what's she called?. . . Oh, very American . . . what? . . . Well yes of course your mother will be disappointed, I mean we both will, but . . . what? . . . later in the year? . . . Good, good, we'll look forward to that. . . Yes, very expensive. No, don't worry, she'll understand. Well have a happy Christmas my boy. . . Yes, we will. 'Bye now. . .'

'So Simon's not coming home after all,' said Alice, with more bitterness than she really felt.

'Now don't take it too hard. He sent all his love and explained exactly why.'

'Money, I suppose.' She wondered if she really was very disappointed, or whether it was just a useful excuse to let out some of her anger. These days Peter's unremitting kindness did not give her the chance. Most of the time it was hard to know what she really felt about anything.

'Far from it. It sounds as though he's doing better than ever. They're threatening to make him a partner or something, so he doesn't want to blow his chances by taking too much time off. They're very busy apparently.'

'And Christmas? Is he going to spend that in the office too?' She plonked the teapot down on the table and clattered around with cups and saucers.

'Well that's the other thing. There's some girl he's going to spend Christmas with – with her family, he said. She's called Lola,' he laughed. 'God, you can't get more American than that!'

'You really don't seem to mind, Peter, do you?'

'Don't be ridiculous, of course I mind,' he replied, ruffled at such a suggestion. 'But the boy sounded well and happy and I'm delighted he's got himself a girlfriend – it must be pretty serious for him to bother to mention her. And oh yes, he also said that they would probably get over here in the spring – so that's not long to wait is it now?'

'They?'

'Yes, "they" – Simon and this Lola girl. Really Alice, anyone would think you were jealous or something,' he teased. 'I must say, I'm rather intrigued. Perhaps it will be wedding bells in Chicago. How would you fancy that, my dear? Flying over to the States for our son's wedding? Now that would be exciting, wouldn't it?' He slurped his tea.

His high spirits are going to kill me, she thought.

'What an idea, honestly, Peter. Anyway, perhaps we won't like her and then it wouldn't be quite so jolly.'

Peter marvelled for the hundredth time how Alice, once so positive, now leapt to see the dark side of everything. It didn't annoy him, it just made him sad for her.

'I think we can trust our son's judgement,' he said gently. 'Is there a drop of tea left in that pot or have you wolfed the lot?'

· 24 ·

A Family Christmas

With its usual grinding inevitability, Christmas came. Robin and Kate arrived on Christmas Eve and that evening Peter opened the first bottle of champagne.

Alice found it very unnerving to see her daughters again. Guilt at Peter's kindness was now mingled with the sense that she had somehow betrayed her children as well. Robin didn't help matters by saying, after a feast of smoked salmon, caviar and champagne:

'Mum, I've been dreaming about your truffles. . .' Peter and Kate burst out laughing. . . 'No, seriously, Kate,' she grinned, 'for the last few nights I've been counting truffles in my sleep. Oh, go on. Can't we break the habit of a lifetime and have some tonight. If I have to wait until after lunch tomorrow I think I shall die – and I certainly won't sleep.'

'Robin you are utterly ridiculous,' said Kate. 'And I simply can't understand why you're not the size of an elephant. You've already eaten more than the rest of us put together. If I had a truffle I think I should pop.' She felt the waistband of her skirt cutting in uncomfortably into her stomach and secretly undid a button. Kate, while far from fat, was plump. With her father's moon face she managed – no matter what she wore – to have the round look of a bossy schoolmistress. Looking from one daughter to the other, Alice thought how strange it was that she should feel so

141

detached from the two of them. Once she would have known how many breaths they took in a minute, when they last hiccoughed and what made them smile. Now I don't know anything, she thought, and they know nothing about me. It was not a pleasant sensation either, to realize that she did not like the plump, matronly look of her eldest, nor the messy, arty look of her youngest, whose numerous chains and bangles round her wrists and neck meant that when she moved she sounded like a badly tuned doorbell. She now jangled off to the kitchen in search of truffles.

'Robin, I'm afraid you're going to be disappointed anyway,' called Alice, 'I simply didn't have time to make any this year.'

Robin appeared immediately in the doorway. 'You didn't make any truffles. . . Oh Mum, you're joking. . .'

'For goodness sake,' put in Peter, coming to Alice's rescue, 'your mother has been extremely busy and very tired. We bought some truffles instead – from Harrods, so they might even be almost as good. Go on, get the box and we'll all have some with our coffee.'

It was not an easy family reunion. Kate and Robin had never got on particularly well and, now they were older, their differences were more marked than ever. Kate disapproved of her younger sister's happy-go-lucky existence in Birmingham and made no pretence otherwise. Robin, on the other hand, thought Kate looked more like a frumpy old teacher every time she saw her. Not even going to Madrid – a move which had amazed Robin – seemed to have helped. Kate was still as square and critical as ever; full of snide remarks about unemployed actors living off the state and revelling in their idleness. What's more, she had eyed Robin's clothes which such obvious disdain that it had taken all the younger sister's will-power not to explode within the first few minutes of getting home. What stopped her was partly the determination not to ruin Christmas and partly her Theory About Kate. This theory, formulated over many years, was that her elder sister's unpleasantness stemmed from jealousy of her: her freedom, her open nature, her boyfriends and, most certainly of all, her stick-like figure. So for the most part she resisted the temptation to swipe back, silently thankful that she was as she was, and sensing that her 'knowing' look infuriated Kate far more than any words ever could. In fact – though she would not have admitted it for the world – her slimness was the result of considerable hard work, heartache and indigestion. She would go through days when she binged on chocolate, doughnuts, biscuits and doorstep sandwiches of chocolate spread and sugar; followed by periods of starvation. But the myth had grown up – in the family anyway – that she was one of those lucky people who could eat exactly what she wanted and get away with it. It was an image that appealed to her – the instinctive eater who manages to burn up all the calories without a care in the world – and so she did her best to foster it.

The not uncommon loathing of family gatherings comes in most cases from the pressure on everyone to perform. In the Hatton household, their small numbers made the spotlight on each more intense. From that point of view alone it was a shame, thought Alice, that Simon had not made it after all. He was so good at jollying them all along, being genuinely relaxed, extremely witty and a great peace-maker. It had always been him who brought about the reconciliations between the girls, she now recalled, as she stabbed the turkey with a skewer to see if it was cooked.

'Lunch will be another hour at least, I'm afraid,' she called.

'Don't worry, we'll start on the booze anyway,' came Peter's voice, in the grim tone of one determined to have a good time.

They were all having to work very hard at enjoying themselves. All of them were 'between roles' – as parents, lovers, daughters, friends, sisters. In a family where things had been running smoothly and openly, it would have been difficult enough to make the various transitions. But in the case of the Hattons, where what had become important to each of them was a secret from the others, it created a strain so thick it was almost tangible. Only Peter had gone halfway towards being honest – with Alice at least – but he was so terrified of the girls realizing how depressed their mother was, that he was as much to blame as the rest of them. A chaos of superficiality reigned. A chaos of unspoken thoughts and fears. They flew around the house like evil spirits, poisoning the air but secure in their invisibility.

· 25 ·

Trying to Talk

Robin had eaten too much. Her jeans felt tighter than she ever remembered them. Putting one last truffle in her mouth, she resolved to starve herself for at least forty-eight hours. Kate was off the next day, so it would not mean losing face.

The Hattons, like millions of families across the world, had been saved by the television. Having gone through the motions of communication during the first evening and over lunch, they could now collapse in front of a series of films which they had all seen before and which they all claimed to be dying to see again. There they remained, more or less motionless, stuffed with food, until closedown.

'Are you sure I can't give you a lift to the station tomorrow, Kate?' said Peter, switching off the set, 'it's awfully early to go hunting for a taxi.'

'No thanks, Dad. I'll be fine. I'll take the bus anyway, I expect.'

'How early is early?' asked Robin.

'Too early for you, that's for sure,' said Kate with a laugh.

'How do you know?'

'Well, how does eight o'clock sound?'

'Oh God, that early. I'll say goodbye now, then. Good luck with everything. Have a good time in Wales. Write

145

soon and all that sort of thing.' She pecked Kate on the cheek.

'I'll be back in Madrid by February. You must come and stay this year.' There was not much conviction in her voice.

'Yes, I'd love to,' said Robin, equally unconvincingly. She shot her sister a parting smile and went up to bed.

'I expect you'll be up, won't you?' Kate looked at her parents.

'Yes, yes, we'll be up of course, my love,' said Peter, 'but only if I'm asleep within the next five minutes. Sleep well, Kate.'

'Goodnight, darling,' said Alice. 'I think I'm as tired as your father.' She kissed her daughter and turned to follow Peter up the stairs.

'Mum.' Alice stopped and looked back.

'Yes, darling?'

'I . . . well . . . is everything all right? I mean you do seem very tired.'

Alice was almost tempted to tell her the truth. What a relief it would be, to turn to another woman, to say 'no, I'm not all right. I love a man who is tiring of me and my husband is suffocating me with attention. Help me find a way out.' But it was her daughter. It would shatter their normal lines of communication. It might shatter Kate; and it would certainly start something new for which Alice did not feel ready. Added to that, Kate's dowdiness, the hint of loneliness in her own eyes, did little to inspire faith in her as a confidante. All these thoughts flashed, half-formulated, through Alice's mind as she slowly arranged her facial muscles into a large smile and answered:

'Darling how sweet of you to notice. But that's all it is, honestly. I've just been overdoing it with the usual pre-Christmas whirl. Nothing that a few good nights' sleep won't put right.' She kissed Kate again, to put the seal on her reassurance, and wished her goodnight for the second time.

'Thank you for a lovely Christmas,' said Kate, her voice sounding sad.

'It was lovely to have you,' replied Alice, putting out the light.

· 26 ·

The Letter

Kate had gone – to spend a couple of days with a girlfriend in Wales before flying back to Spain; Peter was back at work; and only nine days remained until the first Tuesday in January. Robin was still at home. Having originally said that she would stay for just a couple of days, she now showed no signs of moving. Neither Peter nor Alice wanted to question her too closely about her plans in case she should take offence. Indeed, since Christmas Day she had been increasingly edgy, refusing to eat properly and sitting for hours flipping through magazines and drinking countless cups of coffee. Alice could not help thinking back to how different it had been the last time she and her youngest daughter had shared the house together: Robin on an endless merry-go-round of aerobics, dance and acting classes, between which she would dash home for lunch or to drag her mother off to a matinee or – more often – to look at some expensive article of clothing for which she wanted to borrow money. Harum-scarum and demanding – but so full of life and fun.

Alice had changed too, of course. Having her youngest daughter at home did not induce the old desire to rush round after her, pandering to her every need. She was as fond of her as ever – nothing could change that. But the new experience – brought on by Robin's departure – of having time to herself had not only made her lonely, it had made her selfish. Alice had got used to organizing her day to suit her own moods. With her daughter loafing around the house, she could no longer indulge in such luxuries. Added to that, Robin's presence acted like a niggling shadow of guilt. With her around she found she was unable to even think about Edward properly. At a time when she wanted to be alone to rally her thoughts, to prepare for the reunion with her lover, she found her listless, sprawling daughter an annoying distraction – a distraction which interrupted the rhythm of her thoughts like loud music or the drip of a tap. And daring to think such things about Robin only made her feel guiltier than ever.

Alice's life, as a wife and a mother, was now nothing more than a front – a thick wall of domesticity behind which her other existence lay hidden like a jewel in a safe. She bustled round mindlessly, following a routine from which she no longer drew any pleasure or comfort and feeling irritated by the slightest things.

'Robin, I'm sorry, darling, but I'm going to have to ask you exactly what you're doing?' she finally blurted out one morning, after hoovering round Robin's feet, piles of magazines and a full ash-tray without managing to provoke any response at all. Robin had not even moved.

'I thought I was spending my Christmas holidays with you,' she said sarcastically, 'but if I'm getting in your way or anything. . .'

'Robin for goodness sake. It is precisely because I knew you would say that, that I have been putting off mentioning it. I just wondered how long you are planning to stay, that's all.'

Robin gave a long-suffering sigh and started idly flipping over the pages of a magazine.

'Surely that's not so much to ask, is it?'

'Why do you always have to have everything just so? You and Dad. Why can't you just let things happen? Life's more fun that way, you know. None of this stupid bother

149

about what is supposed to be happening second by bloody second.'

Exercising considerable restraint, Alice chose to ignore her daughter's rudeness. Instead she said, cleverly she thought: 'It doesn't look to me as if you're having much fun.' With a wrench she saw Robin's bottom lip beginning to tremble. Should she go over to her, she wondered? Or would that only make things worse?

'Darling, you haven't been outside for days. Do you think a little fresh air might help?'

'Yes,' said Robin fiercely, pitting all her throat muscles against the urge to cry. Alice could see the veins standing out in her neck with the effort of it. Without thinking she went over to her and tried to put her arm round her. Robin shook her off aggressively and marched into the hall. Without even a look at her mother she slung her large llama shawl – which Alice loathed for its hairiness, its dirty tassles and smell of stale cigarettes – over her shoulders and went outside, slamming the front door behind her.

Of course Alice was worried about Robin. It was not like her to mooch around snapping at everybody, sulking and refusing to eat. A year ago she would have been more worried, however. Now, her own problems weighed more heavily on her mind than those of her daughter. So she wrote it off as a late adolescent phase that was bound to pass in time and about which she could do nothing. Her main feeling, as the front door banged shut, was relief at having an hour or so to herself.

A few minutes later she was lying on the sofa, a steaming mug of coffee and two digestive biscuits perched on her stomach, luxuriating in the first opportunity for many days to think about the approaching meeting with Edward. I will have to appear strong and independent, she told herself, if I am to get things back to how they were. She began to imagine what she would wear, how she might tell him of Peter's astonishing declaration of love in a way that would make him laugh. . . .

150

A noise from the hall gave her such a jolt that she spilt some coffee on her skirt as she swung her legs to the ground and sat bolt upright.

'Is that you, Robin?'

All was silent. Feeling nervous, she quietly put down her coffee, brushed the crumbs from her skirt, and went to investigate. There was no one in the hall or kitchen. Nothing was amiss. Except, that is, for the presence of a small white envelope on the doormat, blocking out the W of the 'WELCOME'. Alice's heart missed a beat even before she had picked it up and recognized the handwriting. It was a letter from Edward. More grateful than ever for being on her own, she tried to quell the premonitions of disaster that came rushing over her in tidal waves. Holding the envelope as one might a letter-bomb, she went back to the sitting room and placed it on the table. There she sat looking at it, trying to equip herself for whatever it might say, while she slowly finished her coffee. Her appetite for the digestives seemed to have gone.

In the end it was the fear that Robin would come back that made her force her trembling fingers towards the envelope. It smelt of his after-shave. Or was it just her imagination? Taking a deep breath, she tore it open and plunged in:

'My dear Alice,' it began. 'By the time you get this I shall be in Portugal. You may remember my mentioning that Carol's parents had a villa there. I may as well get it over with straight away and tell you that I shall be there with Carol. We are trying to make a second go of it. While I know this will make you sad, I know too that you will in a way be glad if I am able to make my marriage work. I can recall now so many of the talks we had about being married and why it was so hard when it could have been so easy.

When I last saw you, I did not know this was going to happen, I swear it. Otherwise I should have told you to your face. But the 'reconciliation' – for want of a better word – came

151

quite out of the blue and right in the middle of Christmas. I knew you would be busy with all the children being home and that it would therefore be difficult either to get in touch with you or to arrange a meeting. Hence this letter, which smacks of cowardice, I know.

What else can I say? To talk about the pleasure of knowing you would be both painful and pointless. You know as well as I what good times we shared.

I can only hope that you and Peter will find a new way to love each other, as Carol and I have done. Strange that our marriages drew us together just as they must now draw us apart.

Take good care of yourself, Alice.

With fondest love, Edward.'

All Alice's forebodings about Edward's change of heart did nothing to help her cope with the reality of it. Reading his letter cast her back to that desolate morning when Robin had left and she had realized for the first time that she was completely alone. The fact of returning – of having tried and failed to find comfort in another man, another love, another life – made the desolation so much worse. It was familiar territory; only now she knew that, as well as being hard and barren, it was endless.

Although the letter was typically kind and polite, it deliberately left no room for hope. She could not know, however, that it was dishonest; that Carol had returned and won him back before their last meeting. Edward, being genuinely honest, had thought long and hard over whether to tell her the full truth. In the end it was compassion that stopped him. The chances of Alice ever finding out about the overlap were so remote; and the knowledge, he knew, would cause her so much additional pain, that he could not bring himself to do it. Somewhere too, at the back of his romantic, slightly arrogant mind, lay the desire to leave her honourably, as it were, with his image intact.

Alice heard the front door bang and footsteps coming up the stairs. Then came various sounds of running water from the bathroom and finally the slamming of Robin's bedroom door. She had no idea how long Robin had been gone, nor how many minutes had passed since she had thrown herself on to her bed. After reading Edward's letter once, she had burnt it – in a saucepan lid in the kitchen. For a few seconds the paper had flared into strong yellow flames, before sinking quickly into a pile of black curls. Alice had poked at these with the used match, reducing them to a tiny heap of grey ashes which she tipped into the pedal-bin. She had then washed off the brown burn-marks in the lid and gone upstairs to bed.

When Peter got home from work a couple of hours later, he found the house so dark and quiet that at first he thought Robin and Alice had gone out together somewhere. But then strains of music came floating down from Robin's room, so he knew she was in. He discovered Alice when, having read the morning mail, he went upstairs to change. Switching on the light, he was amazed to see her lying on the bed with a pillow over her head.

'Alice, my goodness . . . are you all right?' He went immediately over to her bedside and gently lifted the pillow. She stared up at him wide-eyed and then blinked slowly, like an owl.

'Hello, Peter. Could you turn the main light off, do you think? I've got a very bad migraine and just need to lie in the dark for a while. I don't feel up to eating or cooking anything, so I'm afraid you and Robin will have to fend for yourselves. Perhaps you could go out and eat. And now I think I will try and get some sleep.' With that, she put the pillow back over her face.

Peter was too surprised to say anything. He squeezed her hand, made what he hoped were a few comforting noises and tiptoed out of the room, turning off the light as he went.

153

· 27 ·

New Year's Eve

The prospect of a new year did not seem to be doing much
to raise the spirits of either his wife or his daughter, Peter
noted sadly. Both of them were wandering around as if
they knew for certain that the approaching twelve months
contained an unremitting series of catastrophes. Alice, he
knew, was still suffering from an acute attack of migraine,
but Robin had less justification for wearing such a long face.
Coming home to their silent glumness on the eve of 31st
December, was almost funny.

'Now look, something has got to be done about you two,'
he said. 'I have never seen anything like it.' His tone was
mock-scolding, like a mother telling off a child whose crime
is more amusing than serious. Nothing could quash Peter's
spirits these days. He saw everything in the light of a
delightful challenge, for which he had limitless energy and
enthusiasm. They had received a long letter from Simon,
apologizing for letting them down over Christmas and
telling them much more of the Lola girl, about whom he
was clearly serious. This struck Peter as excellent news and
plans of going to America really were taking shape in his
mind. It was a place he had always been curious about, but
never had a good enough pretext to visit. It would do Alice
the world of good he was sure. Added to that, there was
marvellous news on the work front: one of the other senior
partners was leaving and the decision had been taken not to

replace him. Peter was to move into the spacious office which would fall vacant, and all the partners could consequently look forward to receiving greater slices of the practice's profits. The only existing problem in his life was how to cheer up the ladies.

'Right. I have a plan,' he said. 'Both of you are to go upstairs this instant and put on your best frocks. Brush your hair and all that sort of thing, because we're going out.'

Robin groaned and Alice gave him a pained look.

'Those are orders. If you refuse to change we're going out anyway – even if I have to drag you both bodily to the car myself.' He turned to Robin. 'For God's sake try and perk up a little bit. Your mother's not feeling well, I know, but I really don't know what's got into you, Robin.' But, having started to vent some of his frustration on her, he quickly thought better of it. 'Come on love,' he said more gently, 'it's New Year's Eve.' He patted her head and added, 'try not to smile now, you might enjoy it.' This had been one of the things he had always said to the children when they were small and sulking. That and a bit of tickling had never failed to get a smile out of Robin's dimply face. She now managed to stretch the sides of her mouth slightly – but it looked more like a prelude to crying than smiling.

'OK, Dad. I'll go and change.' She slouched out of the room and they could hear the slow, heavy steps with which she dragged herself upstairs.

'Have you any idea what on earth is the matter with her?' said Peter, sounding truly concerned.

'It's just a phase I expect – late adolescence, you know,' said Alice wearily.

'One hell of a phase if you ask me. Is she worried about anything? Hasn't she said anything to you?'

'Peter, I've told you. I don't know.' Since receiving the fateful letter from Edward, Alice's politeness towards her husband had slipped noticeably. The migraine made a

155

good excuse. But now Peter gave her such a hurt look that she added:

'I think she might be worried about her weight. She does look ever so slightly fatter than usual and she's eating very erratically – starving herself one minute and then gorging her way through all sorts of extraordinary things the next. I have tried talking to her. But you can see how she is for yourself. I suppose if it goes on much longer we might suggest she sees Dr Parks. It could be glandular fever or something. I believe that makes you very depressed.'

Peter was relieved to hear this. Partly because it was a possible explanation and partly because it was the longest speech he had got out of Alice since the migraine came on.

'I'm sure you're right, my darling. You always were right about the children.' He kissed her on the forehead. 'Are you going to get changed now? I'm quite serious about taking you both out. I think it will do the world of good.'

Alice could see he was determined to carry out the idea. Since the only supper she had planned was left-overs, she could think of no reason to put up any more resistance.

When they both came back down, half an hour later, Peter was holding two long glasses of creamy yellow liquid in his hands, looking pleased with himself:

'Homemade Pina Coladas – I'm half way through mine and it's delicious.'

Alice and Robin had no option, but to accept the drinks.

'And here's the first toast of the evening: "To the coming year. May it be the best year of all of our lives!" '

'To the coming year', mumbled the ladies. And they all chinked glasses.

Due to the effect of the cocktails on two empty stomachs, followed by aperitifs before dinner, the meal itself turned out to be surprisingly successful. Robin, especially, opened up for the first time in days, showing some of the liveliness and humour that normally governed her character. Even Alice managed to smile during some of her daughter's

156

accounts of behind-the-scene disasters in the apparently chaotic world of fringe theatre in Birmingham.

To celebrate everybody's new-found high spirits Peter ordered a bottle of champagne to accompany their desserts. By the time the bill came Robin was very giggly.

'Oh God, he's brought it in a box!' she gasped, stuffing her napkin in her mouth, as the waiter placed a huge box in front of Peter, its lid inlaid with elaborate swirls of silver and mother-of-pearl. 'How ghastly! And why so big? I suppose because their bills are always so bloody enormous!' She could hardly get the words out she was laughing so much.

'Sh, honestly Robin,' said Alice, letting out an involuntary giggle herself.

Peter felt a little more sober when his eyes focused on the bill. He was extremely pleased with the way the evening had gone, however, and consoled himself with this thought as he placed a wad of notes in the box.

Robin waved to their waiter as they left the reastaurant and wiped an imaginary tear from her eye with exaggerated movements.

'Such a nice boy,' she said. 'Shame about the. . .'

'Now come on, Robin. Save your theatrics for the stage,' said Peter laughing in spite of himself, 'or at least until we get home.'

'Home? Home? But the night is young,' she said, skipping off down the pavement ahead of them. 'We must go on and on and on. . .' She danced off round the corner.

'Oh dear,' said Alice. 'I think she may be just a little. . .'

'We're all just a little,' put in Peter, 'and it's not doing us any harm at all.'

'I found the car, I found the car,' sang Robin, reappearing. Obviously inspired by the sound of her voice, she then went on in shrill but tuneful tones:

> 'I'm Diana Dors and I'm a movie star,
> I've got a cute cute figure

157

And a motor car.
I got the hips, lips,
Legs in style
I'm Diana Dors and I'm a movie star.'

She waggled her bottom and pouted her lips as she sang, hopping out of her parents' way as they tried to restrain her.

'That was wonderful, darling,' said Peter, thankful that the street was virtually empty, 'and now let's all get in the car you've so cleverly found for us.'

She went very quiet suddenly and sidled up to him like a little girl.

'Can we have more champagne when we get home, Daddy?' she said, looking up at him from under her long eyelashes.

'I think we might, my darling.' He kissed her nose and she got into the car obediently.

'I think we ought to see in the New Year properly, don't you, Alice my love? There's only half an hour to go till midnight and we've still got one bottle of champagne left over from Christmas.'

'Hurray! Champagne!' called Robin from the back seat, on which she was lying fully stretched, her stockinged feet pressed up against the window.

'Lovely idea,' murmured Alice, 'but I feel so sleepy suddenly.' Indeed it felt as if troops of invisible fairies were dancing along her eyelids, their tiny feet tickling her skin and their combined weight forcing the lids down like shutters. She rubbed her eyes and opened the window to get a blast of the cool night air. Robin's feet appeared at her left shoulder. She tickled them affectionately, causing squeals of delight from behind.

'Honestly, I can't take you two anywhere,' said Peter happily.

They made a strange drinking trio that night. Robin lay on the floor, her hands behind her head, her champagne glass balanced precariously on her stomach. Alice had thrown herself on to the sofa, where she was propped amongst the cushions like some latter-day Cleopatra. Her hair – which for several weeks she had been allowing to return to its original steely grey – was tucked severely behind her ears, curling under them and inwards to frame her jaw-line; she had kicked her shoes off and her skirt was half hitched above her knees. Beside her, Peter sprawled in his favourite armchair, his feet on the coffee table and a big grin on his face. Not even the knowledge that his thatch of hair had gone completely awry – it hung down the wrong side of the absurdly low parting, exposing the dreaded bald patch – could disturb his sense of tranquillity. Centre-stage was the champagne bottle, which had been uncorked on the stroke of midnight and quickly drained of its contents. Reflected in its green sides were ugly, distorted images of the three figures who had turned to it for a final boost to their spirits.

Peter had by now joined Alice in the sleepy phase of over-indulgence. Robin – perhaps because of a younger blood system – was still several stages behind them. Although not as lively as on leaving the restaurant, she was still very talkative.

'Men, horrible things. I hate them. Don't you, mother?' she hooted with laughter.

'Yes, darling, quite horrible,' said Alice. She gave Peter a prod. 'Wake up, darling, your daughter is about to tell us why men are so horrible. Something I knew already but have never fully understood.' Peter reluctantly opened his eyes, too bleary to realize that a new, sour note had entered his happy evening. As yet it hung over their heads, like a drop of poison, gathering head before falling.

'They fuss and flatter, fuss and flatter till a girl collapses in adoration at their feet. Like an aeroplane diving into a crash landing.' She gave her impression of an aeroplane doing just this by making a squeaky, whining noise through her teeth and flapping her arms in the air. Since

159

she was still lying on the floor, the performance bore an uncanny resemblance to someone having an epileptic fit.

'And then, of course, the crash comes. You crawl around maimed for a bit, begging for life and love, and then finally give up. Flop. Dead.' She twitched and then lay still.

'Robin, what are you talking about? You've lost me completely,' said Alice, genuinely disappointed that her daughter had not explained her thoughts on men better.

'You never had me at all,' came Peter's slurred voice from the depths of the armchair.

'What I am talking about,' said Robin, now enunciating the words in an unnaturally crisp, brisk manner, 'is Mr Bob Tupper, comedian extraordinaire – comedian of life, that is, not stage. Darling, darling Bob. Just couldn't keep his hands off, could he? What was it we used to call his problem at school? Oh yes, I remember. . .' she paused to giggle, '. . .W.H.T. That was it! All the boys in our school plays used to have it. W.H.T. You don't know what that stands for do you, Mum? Well I'll tell you. It's jolly simple really. It stands for Wandering Hand Trouble. It's fine and dandy of course when the hands you want wander over the places you want. But Bob's trouble was that they wandered all over me and various other lithe little bodies as well. Not always female ones either.'

'Oh Robin, my darling. . .' Alice was horrified.

Even Peter, who had been struggling with a gravitational pull towards oblivion, was jerked back to consciousness by these words. Dimly he sensed that more horrors were about to be revealed. He wanted either to stop her or to get out of the room. But the muscles controlling his mouth seemed to have solidified and his legs felt paralysed with tiredness.

'Oh no, but it's funny really. Listen to this. I put up with it. Even though I knew, I put up with it. Have you ever heard anything so hilarious?' Her eyes blazed with hurt and anger. 'But then came the special surprise. Bob's Christmas present to me. He let me find him in bed with his latest starlet – Fiona Waring, if you're interested – on purpose. What daring! What imagination! What pigshit!'

All Alice and Peter could do was stare open-mouthed at Robin. She had by now raised herself from the floor and was sitting with her long legs folded elastically in front of her, her hands clutching her knees and her eyes staring widely back into the horrified faces of her parents.

'He actually wanted me to find them together. And do you know why? Because all other ways of getting rid of me had failed!' Her laugh cracked round the drawing room, hard and hollow. 'Yes, Robin Hatton, the devoted moron, had insisted on forgiving him every time, on giving him the benefit of the doubt, on "understanding" his multifarious urges. So the poor darling had no option. The only way to kill me off was to shatter my pride so completely that not even I – I with all my capacity for self-mortification – could go crawling back for more.' She swigged the last mouthful of champagne in her glass and grabbed the bottle from the table.

'Haven't you got any more of this stuff?' She waved it around like a weapon. Peter just shook his head, his mouth still frozen.

'Darling, I know. Believe me, I know.' Alice swayed forward from the sofa with an air of confidentiality. She wanted so badly to tell Robin that she too had been abandoned. If they had been alone she would have done. But, in spite of her befuddled state, she could not bring herself to do it with Peter in the chair beside her. Perhaps if he had fallen asleep. . .

'Are you asleep, dear,' she said in a loud voice. Peter, who had his eyes shut, shook his heady slowly.

'We must talk alone, Robin. There's so much I can tell you that will make you see that I know so well what you are suffering. You're so right, my darling,' she went on in a lower voice, 'it's men, they're horrible.' She spat the last word in a loud whisper of disgust and promptly fell back into the cushions.

161

'But I haven't told you the final joke yet. I want you both to hear it. You see Bob had yet another trick up his sleeve – a secret, secret present, that I would only discover after I'd packed my things.'

They both continued staring at her, wondering what more humiliations she could possibly be about to reveal.

'This one was not so much a Christmas present as a gift for the New Year.' Robin was enjoying having such a spellbound audience. She drained the last gulp in Alice's glass and went on: 'Because I only found out about it yesterday – found out for sure, that is.'

'Oh Robin, no.' Alice had already seen where the story was leading.

'What do you mean, "Robin, no", like that,' spluttered Peter, finding his voice through sheer infuriation. 'What are you talking about, Robin?'

'I'm pregnant, Dad. That's what I'm talking about.' Her voice, so bold before, was now small and sad. She hung her head, studying the empty glass in her hands. 'I am pregnant. Bob Tupper is the father. And I am never going back to Birmingham again.' The thin champagne glass, which she had been gripping so furiously, suddenly broke, its sides snapping under the pressure of her fingers.

'Fuck. Oh, fucking hell.' She crooned the words, rocking slowly backwards and forwards over her bleeding hands.

'Robin. . .!' Alice started forward to comfort her and only then noticed the shattered glass in her lap and the small razor-like cuts on her fingers. The shock made her sober.

'My darling heart, what have you done? My poor darling. Get up. It's all right. Come on. There's my lamb. Come on now. Let's wash your hands. It will be all right. That's it. My poor, poor darling.' So Alice, rising spectacularly to meet the crisis, coaxed her daughter now sobbing breathlessly, out of the sitting room. At the door she looked back over her shoulder at Peter, who was staring blankly at the pattern of broken glass and tiny blood-drops which marked the spot where Robin had been sitting.

162

'Could you have a go at clearing that up do you think, Peter? I'm going to put Robin to bed. Cold water is the best thing for blood.'

Like a sleep-walker, Peter obediently got up from the chair and went to look for a cloth and a dustpan.

Half an hour later, just as he was getting into bed, Alice put her head round their bedroom door.

'She doesn't want to be left alone. I'm going to make up the spare bed and sleep in there with her. We can talk in the morning. I've already got my things. Good night, Peter.'

'Alice. . .' he began, but she was already shutting the door.

· 28 ·

Possibilities

The next morning Peter was woken with a steaming cup of
tea. Alice looked annoyingly refreshed and active. His head
ached terribly. He watched her draw the curtains and
screwed his eyes up at the unwelcome intrusion of light. At
first he could not remember why he felt depressed other
than because he was hung-over. Then the memory of
Robin's revelation flashed into his mind like the stab of a
knife. He groaned.

'How's Robin?' he managed.

'Asleep.' Alice carried on busying herself about the
room, picking up Peter's clothes – which he had thrown
carelessly to the floor the night before – and folding them
away. 'I gave her one of my Mogadon tablets last night, so I
expect she'll be out for a while yet. The poor lamb can't
have got too much sleep recently with all that to worry
about on her own. But still, thank God she's told us. With
our help she will be all right.'

'Yes. I don't suppose she has enough money saved to
manage on her own, that's for sure.'

Alice now stood at the door, a bundle of dirty washing in
her arms, her face flushed from all the scurrying around she
had been doing.

'We'll talk about it over breakfast, shall we?' she said
brightly.

'Yes of course. Nothing much for me thank you – I'm

feeling a little delicate. Heaven knows why you're so perky. Have you discovered a new hangover cure you're not telling me about?' He clutched his head as he swung his legs out of bed.

'I just slept very well, that's all. And anyway there's too much to do to have a hangover.' With that she rushed off to put the washing machine on and make breakfast. Peter may not have thought he wanted much to eat, but fried eggs and bacon were, in Alice's view, the best cure for a bad head.

The cooked breakfast did do Peter a lot of good. After eating everything on his plate, a jugful of coffee and two pieces of toast spread thickly with butter and Alice's homemade marmalade, he felt almost ready to talk about Robin. Alice, knowing her husband well, had bided her time, letting him recover, before launching into the subject weighing so heavily on both their minds.

'Thank God she told us,' she said again, finally sitting down and pouring herself the last of the coffee.

'Thank God indeed. As for that Bob Tupper character . . . if I ever get my hands on him . . .'

'Peter, for goodness sake, he is the least of our worries. You heard what Robin said: it's all over. She's never going back to him – or Birmingham. All we have to concern ourselves about is our daughter.'

'Yes, but I heard what else she said – in spite of the wretched booze,' he put his hand to his temple, suddenly recalling his hangover. 'That man ought to be locked up. A villain if ever I saw one. What can Robbie have seen in him I wonder? I never liked him in the slightest.'

'Well you put up a pretty good show of liking him when he came to stay, is all I can say,' said Alice, remembering her own doubts after that weekend and how Peter had scorned her for being over-protective.

'Plying him with drink, being all man-to-man – he must have been laughing up his sleeve. I bet the fathers of his other women – and men for that matter – don't treat him like that.'

165

'Alice!' It was the mention of the men which shocked Peter and she knew it.

'We might as well face it all now. Robin's got to and so must we.'

'I like the way you blame me.' Peter's hangover was feeling worse by the second. 'I was only nice to him for Robin's sake. I only did it for her.' He reached across the table and grabbed Alice's hand suddenly.

'Don't let's argue now' he whispered. 'It's all so awful anyway.' Still gripping her hand, he went on urgently: 'This is the sort of time when we should be able to draw closer together. You have been marvellous, darling – looking after her last night, not panicking at all. Given how tired you've been and with the migraine and everything I am so impressed – and so grateful.'

Alice looked at him in surprise. 'Yes . . . well I just felt that I knew what to do, how to comfort her. I didn't have to think about it at all.' Thinking about it now, however, she realized that, in a way, she had been secretly enjoying the drama. Not for any callous reason, but because, for the first time in many months, she had felt needed. Not just half-wanted some of the time. But well and truly needed. If she had not taken control of the situation when she did, heaven knows what would have happened. Peter would probably have passed out from drink and shock, while Robin could easily have staggered to the bathroom and added to the blood by cutting her wrists. Recognizing all this, Alice saw the ridiculous simplicity of it: being necessary made her happy. Her daughter had needed her last night. And when she woke up she would need her still. And with the baby she would need her still more . . .

'The baby, Peter . . .' But he had disappeared to read the newspaper in the lavatory. Alice ground some more coffee beans. They smelt strong and fresh. So not even a family crisis can disrupt Peter's daily ablutions, she marvelled. Although she too could hardly be said to have been traumatized by Robin's revelations – quite the contrary in fact. Her mind was clearer and more confident than it had ever been. As she sat waiting for Peter to reappear, it was not the future which preoccupied her thoughts – on that she felt absolutely clear – but the past.

It was only with her children, she realized, that she had ever felt this need – of them for her. Between her and a man – her mind quickly flitted down her meagre list of conquests: Peter, Horatio, Edward – there had never been anything like it. She quickly discounted Peter and Horatio, since it was love that she was really thinking about. Peter's only need of her was – and always had been – domestic; and Horatio had not needed her at all – except for a little blip to his ego. So it came down to Edward and what she considered to be her only true experience of sexual love. Need had been there all right – in bucketfuls. But it had always come from her: her needing love; her craving demonstrations of affection; her seeking reassurance. Her, her, her. Thinking back now, she could not recall a single occasion when Edward had ever made any similar demands on her. He must have felt them sometimes. Was it just male pride, then? Fear of appearing vulnerable? The difference, she concluded, was confidence. As she had said to Peter, there had been no need to think what to do with Robin to soothe her. She had just known and felt confident that her instincts were right. With the men in her life – including her husband – she had never felt remotely confident about how to behave. She had spent the early part of her marriage, (when she still cared enough to try), and all her time with Edward endeavouring to act as she thought they wanted her to, and – as if it was inscribed in some Manual of Human Life – how she thought she was supposed to act. With these realisations, a minuscule cog in the machinery of Alice's mind altered the way it turned. An imperceptible alteration in itself, but one that would have the power to affect several lives. All Alice knew was that sitting there at the kitchen table, listening to the coffee go into the last orgiastic throes of its cycle, thinking so easily

167

and dispassionately about her problems, she felt wonderful. She could not remember when she had last felt so good. Of course Robin was a worry; but she was so sure of the correct solution, that she hardly needed to think about it. Life is really so simple, she thought.

'About the baby,' she began again when Peter emerged.

'Oh dear, yes. I've been wondering, how much does it cost?'

'How much does what cost?'

'Why the . . .' he gave a glance up the stairs and closed the kitchen door, 'The abortion, of course.'

'What abortion?' Her lips had gone thin and white.

'Alice, you cannot seriously be imagining that Robin should have this child? Dear God, now I've heard everything.'

'Of course she must have it. Of course she must. It is her baby, Peter . . .'

'And that brute's. I suppose you want her to marry him as well, do you?'

'Don't be ridiculous, of course I don't. Like you I wish we could get him imprisoned for what he has put Robin through. It's just that having a child is . . . well, it's the best thing a woman can do,' she ended lamely.

'The best thing a married woman can do, perhaps, but not a young lass who's barely into her twenties and doesn't have a clue what she's going to do with her life. Come on, Alice. Be reasonable.'

'I am being reasonable. We can help her. Heaven knows, we're not short of money. That's what I thought you meant when you said this morning that we could help her. I didn't dream that you meant help her kill the baby.'

Peter refused to rise to the accusation. 'You are getting hysterical, Alice. If you're going to start accusing me of being a child-murderer then we might as well stop this discussion immediately. What I thought we were talking about was Robin and what would be best for her. For a start we haven't any idea what she thinks she's going to do. Unless she said anything to you last night?'

'Of course she didn't. She was far too distraught.'

The familiar sound of the top stair creaking stopped them saying any more. A few moments later Robin appeared, in a long white nightie and with bare feet. Her eyes were small and puffy from sleep; her face dry and pale.

'Mum, have you got anything for a hangover? God, I slept like a corpse.'

'It must have been the Mogadon darling – they tend to do that. Here take this.' She made a glass of some cloudy, fizzy liquid.

'Mogadon? I don't remember taking a Mogadon. I haven't got any.'

'Darling, don't you remember . . .' Alice stopped. She looked at Peter, who buried his head in the paper.

'Remember what?'

'That I gave you a Mogadon last night. And I slept in your room. Didn't you notice the other bed was ruffled?'

'For God's sake, Mum, I've only just woken up. I staggered down here with my eyes shut. Morning, Dad. Do you feel as awful as I do?' She kissed him on the top of the head, tipped away the fizzy drink – of which she had taken one sip – and poured herself a coffee.

'It tends to happen when I really go overboard with the booze. I forget things. All the brain cells get wiped out, you see. It's happened a couple of times before. I always think it would be an awful thing to happen just before an exam – if you celebrate all that swotting with a few drinks, and then obliterate all that you've learnt . . .'

'Robin darling, where do you remember up to?'

'Honestly, mum, it's nothing to worry about. It's happened before, I tell you.' She frowned, as she tried to recall the evening. 'Let me see, I remember the restaurant – where I ate too much, again – then coming out . . . oh yes and I remember lying on the back seat of the car, singing wasn't I? Oh dear was I very dreadful? You look so shocked. Come on, for goodness sake, it was New Year's Eve after all . . .'

'Yes, yes of course it was.' Alice turned to the sink to hide her face. 'And after that, can you remember what happened?'

'After that I must admit that it does begin to get a little hazy. I know Dad opened another bottle of champagne, and I can remember lying on the sitting room floor . . .' both parents held their breath.

'After that . . . no, not a sausage. A complete blank.'

'Do you remember breaking the glass? You cut yourself a bit . . .' prompted Alice.

Robin glanced suddenly at her hands. 'Oh God, so I did. How awful of me. Sorry about that.' She looked at the little cuts across her fingers. 'I must have been pretty far gone. Did we stay up very late?'

There was an awful silence and then Peter and Alice both spoke together.

'No, not really,' said Alice, speaking the loudest.

'Long enough to finish the bottle, that's all,' added Peter, trying, unsuccessfully to sound natural.

'Why on earth did I need a Mogadon, then?'

It was such a simple question. Alice should have seen it coming. In the panic of the moment, she could not bring herself to blurt out the truth. After a couple of agonizing seconds, during which she pretended to be scrubbing hard at something obstinate in the washing-up bowl.

'I read recently that they are good hangover cures, that's why, darling. I took one myself and I feel fine. I slept in your room because I was afraid you might be rather unwell.' Her voice was calm and confident. Her head, meanwhile, had started to throb horribly and her hands were sweating inside the rubber gloves.

Peter got up and left the kitchen, giving Alice a fierce parting look that said 'tell her now.'

'So I was that bad, was I?' Robin whistled quietly. 'As for the Mogadon cure – it must depend on your metabolism or

170

something, because it's certainly done nothing for me.' She tipped some cornflakes into a bowl and went to the fridge. 'Got any yoghurt, Mum – and honey?'

'You loathe yoghurt – and since when have you put honey on cornflakes?' Now she'll tell me. She must tell me now, she thought.

'I've told you – I'm into healthy eating. Anything that's good for me I love.' Having located both things she was now pouring and stirring them liberally over her cereal.

Alice wondered if being healthy was perhaps a sign that she was already thinking about the baby; or whether honey and yoghurt were just pregnancy fetishes. But Robin clearly had no wish to say anything further on the subject. She turned her attention to the paper and crunched noisily on her breakfast, causing a spot of pink to appear on each cheek.

It was all very well Peter giving her meaningful glances, but she had no idea how to start. Robin looked so small and vulnerable: with her hair all tousled from sleep and her small white feet just visible below the long, virginal nightie she was the very picture of innocence. Could it really all be true, she wondered? She felt a terrible urge to protect her daughter, to stop that pale face from crinkling up with misery – at whatever cost. That was one reason why she held her silence. The other was that she wanted Robin to tell her herself. Pride, flattery, memories of how close they had once been – all these things made her hold back. Let Robin tell me in her own good time, she thought, when she knows she's telling me. I'm sure she will. I'm sure of it.

So when Peter came back downstairs and raised his eyebrows at her from behind Robin, she frowned and shook her head. He frowned back at her and said he was going out to do some gardening.

A few minutes later Alice found him viciously cutting a rose bush that had already been pruned down to a few pitiful stumps.

'Peter, there is no need to keep disappearing from rooms

171

throwing me ridiculous looks and winks as you go. I am not going to bring the subject up with Robin because I am sure she will tell me when she is ready.'

'I don't see how you can be so sure, Alice. She's grown very independent over this last year. I feel as if I hardly know her . . .'

That's because you never knew her, Alice wanted to say. But she stopped herself and went on.

'The poor child has only just heard for sure . . .'

'Yes, I wonder which doctor she went to?'

'Goodness knows. But she said it was only yesterday she had found out, didn't she? So of course it is still sinking in. She has to marshal her own thoughts before she can break the news to us. It's only normal.'

'We'll see, shall we?' He clipped another twig off the slaughtered bush and moved along the flowerbed to his next victim. 'I suppose when she realizes she needs money she'll come to us.'

'I don't know how you can be so callous, Peter. Our own daughter – and you say such things.' She stalked back to the house.

· 29 ·

Getting to the Truth

Another day went by and still Robin did not say anything. But she did appear to be in slightly better spirits. Long walks and being helpful about the house were the outward signs of this improvement.

'Any plans for going back to Birmingham?' said Alice lightly, as they were changing the sheets on Robin's bed two days later.

'Nope,' Robin did not look up from tucking in the sheet. 'In fact I've been thinking that I might try something completely different. Don't ask me what,' she quickly went on, 'because I don't know yet. I'm just thinking about it. You don't mind me being at home, do you?'

'Darling heart, of course not. You can stay as long as you like. You know that. Your father and I will always help you in any way we can. You have only to ask.' If Robin read any hidden meaning into these words, she did not show it.

As they moved the bed back into the corner there was a crunch. They both bent down to investigate, but Alice got there first.

'What on earth is this?' She picked up the remains of a small glass contraption that looked something like a miniature egg-timer.

Robin did not say anything, but sat on the bed.

'Robin, I'm talking to you.' Not being familiar with a

173

DIY pregnancy-testing kit, Alice's mind had immediately leapt to drugs. Robin seemed in so much trouble, and so incapable of looking after herself, that it was her first thought. That was why she spoke so sternly.

'Oh God, Mum, give it to me and I'll throw it away.'

'No, I will not give it to you until you tell me exactly what it is.'

'You really don't know, do you?' Robin's tone was scornful.

'I am going to get really angry in a minute. Of course I don't know what the wretched thing is, otherwise I wouldn't be asking, would I?'

'It is a clever little kit you can buy from Boots that tells you whether you're pregnant or not.' Before Alice – overcome with relief – could take her daughter in her arms and say 'darling, I know', Robin continued: 'And you may as well know that the answer is yes, but that it is all going to be all right because I have already arranged to have an abortion.'

'Robin, no!'

Robin thought it was the shock at hearing she was expecting a baby and not her plan to have it aborted that was so horrifying to her mother.

'Look, Mum, it's not that terrible a thing. It happens to lots of people however careful they are. I'm sorry we found this. It was stupid of me not to throw it away. I meant to but forgot. I wasn't going to tell you anything and then you would never have known and never have worried.' In spite of sounding brave, there were tears in her eyes as she looked up to see how Alice was reacting.

'Thank goodness I found out then.' Alice flopped down next to her on the bed. There seemed no point in revealing the full events of New Year's Eve now. It would only put her even more on the defensive. These moments were so important, she knew. How she reacted now could decide everything.

'Don't faint with amazement, Robbie love, but I'm not so terribly shocked as you think. Ancient mums aren't quite so

174

ancient as they sometimes appear. It was just initial surprise that made me shriek at you like that. Shall we go and have a cup of tea and talk about it properly?'

Robin was truly astounded and not a little impressed.

'There's nothing really to talk about – but OK.' It had never crossed her mind that her mother would behave so coolly about the whole thing.

Alice played her part well. She wanted Robin to trust her, to feel she could tell her everything. To do this she intuitively realized two vital things: she must not give a hint of passing judgement, nor should she act as if she understood everything. She and Peter had learnt through experience that pretending to speak the same language as their children only infuriated them. It made them scowl and write their parents off as even more of a pair of old fogies than they had originally thought. In the same way, she could see that she would never get away with acting as if daughters of friends got pregnant all the time. Robin simply would not be fooled by such a front.

All these thoughts raced through her mind, like details of a battle-plan, as she made her way downstairs and put the kettle on.

'Don't tell me anything, if you don't want to, darling. I have always respected your life as your own – you know that, don't you? The last thing I want to do is to interfere. Truly, I don't.'

Robin squirmed a little and mumbled 'I know.'

'But even if we are hopelessly doddery and out of touch – your father and I – we can help sometimes. I mean, just from a money point of view. How . . . I mean I can't help wondering . . . how were you going to pay for the abortion?'

'Friends.' She took a swig of tea and added another heaped spoonful of sugar.

'You were going to borrow it, you mean?'

'Yes. I've got some very good friends, you know.'

'Yes, darling, I'm sure you have. But I can't help thinking

175

it's better to keep loans within the family if one possibly can.' One thing at a time, she told herself. 'Then it doesn't matter so much how long it takes to pay it back.'

'So you would not refuse on principle to lending me money to have an abortion?' Robin looked her mother full in the face for the first time.

Alice stared back boldly. 'Of course not – if that is what you really want. Just as we would lend you money to bring up a child – if that was what you wanted. What I mean is,' she rushed on, before Robin could interrupt, 'that the principle is about helping you, not about anything else.'

Robin looked relieved. She began tracing the grains of wood along the table with her thumbnail.

'Of course I don't much like the idea of having an abortion. But there's absolutely no question of making a go of it with Bob. We . . . well, to speak in clichés, we've split up, you see. Ghastly phrase, isn't it?' She went on studying the table top and Alice did not say anything.

'Anyway, we stopped liking each other. So "el bébé" ' – she patted her stomach – 'and me would be rather on our own. No, I couldn't face it. Jesus, I'm only twenty and there's my career and everything. I'm not sure there's a great demand for pregnant women on stage just at the moment. They tend to prefer stuffing pillows up dresses to the real thing.'

'Robin, honestly.' But they both laughed a little, which made them feel better. 'You wouldn't be on your own though,' said Alice, seizing her chance. 'I – we both – would help you every step of the way. This house is much too big for two as it is. We could turn the spare room back into a nursery – as it used to be – and you could easily get on with your career because I could look after the child for you.' Alice raced on, genuinely enthralled by the vision of what the future could hold. 'Goodness me, twenty isn't that young either. And you've always been very mature for your age.'

'Oh Mum, don't. You're only making things worse.'

176

Robin pushed back her chair, scraping it noisily over the tiled floor. She stood looking out of the kitchen window for a few seconds.

'The thing is, I'm seriously thinking about going to America and trying my luck there. I've got a friend working in New York who says she could help get me started. So you see, coming and living here might not be the answer to anything.'

Alice cursed herself for getting so carried away. She had really blown it now.

'I suppose you'll tell Dad. Yes, I guess you have to. I wonder what he will say? I can't think he'd go exactly wild at the idea of having a squealing brat in the house. Come to think of it, I don't really understand why you're so keen?' She turned to face Alice.

'I am completely anti-abortion, that's why,' she said quickly. 'Unless, perhaps, in very extreme cases where there really isn't a hope that the child could be given a decent start in life.'

'Well I am sorry, then. I had no idea you felt so strongly about it. But like you said a bit ago, it's my life and having a baby would really muck things up right now.'

'I see.' Alice tried not to sound as disappointed as she felt.

'But I think perhaps you were right about the money side of it. None of my friends is exactly rolling in it, so it would make more sense if you and Dad could lend me some.'

'OK. I'll talk to your father about it this evening.' Having made the promise, she could not very well retract it.

When Peter got home, Robin stayed in her room long enough to give her mother time to break the news. Alice told him everything, including her decision not to reveal the full events of New Year's Eve.

'It sounds as though she's being very sensible about the whole thing.'

'Yes, I knew you'd think that.'

'I'm sorry, Dad.' It was Robin, standing in the door, looking pitifully guilty.

'Robin, my poor girl.' Peter went over and hugged her. The movement was clumsy, but it touched Robin, bringing the tears to her eyes. 'I expect you'd like a strong drink, wouldn't you? How about a gin and tonic?' He went back to the drinks cabinet. Alice wanted to protest that drinking was not a good idea for pregnant women, but bit her tongue.

'Thanks, Dad, just a small one – very weak.'

'As your mother said, I know, we will of course lend you the necessary money.' He looked at his shoes, feeling embarrassed.

'Yes, that's great. Thanks.' There was an awkward silence.

'The only thing we both feel, Robin,' – Peter wished he didn't sound like some pompous headmaster – 'is that we should like you to do all this through Dr Parks, so we can make sure the thing is done properly.'

'But I've got the name of a good doctor. I've already spoken to him on the phone and made a preliminary appointment and everything. He's called Dr Thomas and he did sound ever so nice.' She looked pleadingly at her parents. 'I don't think I could face Dr Parks. I've known him too long. I'd be so embarrassed. Please.'

'But this Dr Thomas could be a complete crook or . . . or an amateur,' went on Peter, looking at Alice to give him some support. 'We don't know anything about him, darling.'

'But I do. He's all right. I know he is. The friend who recommended him had exactly the same problem herself you see . . .'

Peter swallowed hard, not wanting to look shocked. 'Well in that case . . . Alice, my love, what do you say?'

'Let Robin do as she will. It's quite clear she has made up her mind.' It doesn't make any difference anyway, she thought.

Robin rushed over and kissed her. 'Thanks, Mum – and you too, Dad. You're both being wonderful. Now you just stay here with your drinks and I'll go and make supper.' She hung around in the doorway for a few seconds, as if trying to think of something else to say. Then disappeared without another word.

'Well that's that I suppose,' said Alice. She picked up some knitting and put the television on. Peter refilled his drink and started on the crossword.

· 30 ·

The Decision

When Robin slammed the door shut and raced upstairs after her trip to the doctor, Alice knew something had gone wrong. After half an hour or so, she ventured up and knocked gently on the bedroom door. There was no reply. She tried opening it, but it was locked.

'Robin, darling, what on earth is the matter?'

Still nothing. She listened hard for the sound of sobbing, but all was quiet. Since it was nearly six o'clock, she decided to wait for Peter to get back before trying any more.

He had rather more success. The moment he called her name and knocked, the door was opened – and immediately shut again, before Alice could follow him in. It was one of the worst snubs of her life. How dare she want to confide in Peter, when he had been one of the laziest, most uninvolved fathers the world had ever known? He did not deserve such confidence. She stormed downstairs, furious at both of them, miserable at being left out.

It seemed an age before Peter found her in the sitting room, knitting aggressively – and far too tightly.

'Poor Robin has had a bit of a shock,' he said, treading the well-worn path to the drinks cabinet.

'I gathered that much. I just don't see why she had to tell you about it and not me.' It was impossible to hide her anger.

180

'She didn't think you'd understand . . .'

'She what? I'm only her mother, for goodness sake. Mothers never understand their children as well as fathers, do they?'

'Alice, there is no need to be like that about it.' He spoke slowly, patiently, as if he was very tired. 'In this particular case it is something that perhaps I can sympathize with more than you.'

'Try me.' She threw her knitting down and folded her arms.

'It seems that she was a lot more pregnant than she thought. That in fact she is over three months pregnant – when she had imagined it was only seven or eight weeks. She had none of the sickness problems you see and er . . . apparently . . . her periods were always irregular anyway.'

Alice was amazed. Not so much at the news – which had not really sunk in – but that Robin had actually been talking about her periods to Peter. Peter! Who had never so much as mouthed the word during the entire quarter of a century they had been married.

'The point is,' he ploughed on, avoiding Alice's eyes, 'that the doctor seems to have advised her against having an abortion. Of course it is perfectly possible medically speaking. But apparently there are some risks involved – although the odds are very much against – of difficulties in having children later on. I don't know all the ins and outs of it. But since Robbie had a few doubts anyway, it's made her feel that she has no choice but to go ahead and have the baby after all.' He paused, giving her time to take all this in.

'Knowing that you were so averse to the idea in the first place – though God knows why – she did not feel that you would be the ideal person to break the news to . . .'

'Whereas you, who had been on her side all along, would.'

'Exactly. A drink?'

'Yes, please – I need one. Well I suppose that's under-standable.' I must not appear too pleased, she thought. But how wonderful; what wonderful, wonderful news. She felt her face flush with excitement. Then a sudden panic.

'She's not going to try for a second opinion or anything, is she?'

'No, I don't think so. She seems to have made up her mind that it would be wrong – although she's hardly happy at having reached such a decision. Poor lass. I wish there was some way we could help her.'

'But Peter there is, of course we can help her. I know it's awful – the whole business is awful – but we can help. In thousands of ways. We can give her money, a home – heavens she'll even have two permanent baby-sitters . . .'

'That's very sweet, Mum, thank you.'

'Robin, I didn't hear you come down the stairs,' she spun round on the sofa, caught off her guard. 'I am sorry, darling, truly I am. I know I was against the whole thing, but even I had been getting used to the idea and thinking that perhaps it was for the best,' she lied.

'Well we're all going to have to get used to something else now, aren't we? Dad, you couldn't pour me one while you're there, could you?' She threw herself into an armchair and lit a cigarette.

'Robin, don't you think, love, that you had better start thinking about giving that up?' Alice could not resist it.

Robin turned her head slowly towards her mother. Holding her eyes, she took a long, strong drag, which she inhaled slowly, deeply, right into her lungs, and then out again.

'Let us get one thing absolutely straight. This is my problem, my pregnancy and – barring accidents – my baby. I shall therefore behave exactly as I see fit. If I wish to drink, I shall drink. If I wish to smoke, I shall smoke. If I decide to go skiing in my eighth month I shall do that too.' Even Robin was slightly overawed by her own audacity.

'I was only trying to be helpful,' mumbled Alice, knowing that she was being infuriating. 'I'll go and lay the table. Dinner's ready when you've both finished your drinks.'

· 31 ·

Robin Relaxes

Much to her surprise, Robin rather enjoyed being pregnant. The strain of twelve months of emotional dramas on and off the stage had left her genuinely exhausted. Otherwise she might have offered more resistance to the bulldozing attentions to which she was subjected by her mother. As it was, she reigned like some child-queen – lavished with favours, but without any true power. But Robin was past caring. She let Alice spoil her as much as she wanted, and sat back to enjoy the ride. After all, none of it would last forever, she told herself.

She blew up like a balloon. Pregnancy – official permission to be fat! The floodgates opened. Years of not allowing herself to be greedy took their revenge in binges of eating that lasted for days. She had gorged herself many times before, of course; but now there were no starvation periods in between.

Alice did nothing to try and check this process. On the contrary, seeing how much Robin was enjoying her food, inspired her to cook more delicious things more often. Her daughter putting on so much weight did not worry her in the slightest. Life was altogether too enjoyable to get concerned about such trivia. For if there was one person who enjoyed these months more than Robin, it was Alice herself. Day after day of heavenly chores – of slaving for someone who really enjoyed and needed it. Hours of planning, preparing and hoping for the baby. Her own pregnancies had not been nearly so much fun. Then she had been alone, less experienced – and of course burdened with the physical aspects as well. Now she had all the enjoyment without any of the discomfort. Robin – especially a fat, immobile Robin – was totally, blissfully dependent on her. She was in fact – although Alice never once thought of it this way – her prisoner. Being fat for the first time in her life, and pregnant but not married, meant that the last thing Robin wanted to do was to venture out of the house. So her physical condition and her situation confined her, with her mother as her only link to the outside world. She did not mind though. What other gaol served up creamy apple flan for dessert and made sure the larder was never out of chocolate Bath Olivers?

Peter, feeling the unhealthiness of the situation, did try half-heartedly to intervene. But, in spite of playing such an important role in events leading up to Robin's reinstatement at home, he now found himself excluded. The house might just as well have had a 'Women Only' sign pinned to the front door. Conversation revolved solely around frills for the cot cover, whether the nursery curtains should match the wall paper or the cushion covers, how many stitches made bootees for a new-born and What The Doctor Had Said. Peter, while he became an unwitting expert on the pros and cons of disposable nappies, was powerless. He tried only once to influence what was going on. Noticing the bloating effect of Robin's slothfulness, he suggested that she start swimming at the local indoor pool as a form of healthy exercise and a way of getting out of the house. Robin went very sulky and Alice kicked him under the table. Later he found himself being severely reprimanded for being so tactless and for making Robin feel guilty. Pregnancy, explained Alice, was the one time when women should relax completely, do exactly as they pleased and enjoy feeling special. Any upsets in such a programme could affect the baby – if not physically then at least mentally, she claimed. Since, between them, Alice and Robin had read every book on pregnancy written in the history of mankind, Peter had not felt in a position to argue.

Instead he found himself spending a lot of time alone again and wishing more than ever that Robin had not got herself into such a mess. Before Christmas he had felt as if he and Alice had been on the verge of a new, wonderful – and totally unexpected – phase in their life together. Now she hardly had time for him at all. He was not really jealous – in fact he was pleased to see her so happy again; but what good was such happiness if he could feel no part of it? He resolved to bide his time. Let the wretched baby be born. Then a little money would set Robin up on her own and he could have his wife back. An elegant old-age of mutual affection and respect, spent visiting children, holidaying and eating good meals had started forming like some hazy vision of hope. He would close his eyes, shutting out the pin-cushions and knitting patterns, and indulge in some secret planning for an early retirement.

Action Stations

When the labour pains started, they came so quickly that Alice could hardly count any gap between them. She rang the hospital immediately and explained that the birth seemed imminent.

'But how many minutes are there between the contractions, Mrs Hatton?' asked the voice in a bored way for the second time.

'I have explained already. They are coming too quickly. There's hardly a minute between them.' Alice was desperate. 'I suggest you send an ambulance.' She was doing up her shirt and pulling on shoes as she spoke. It was four o'clock in the morning and she could hear Peter offering what help he could to Robin next door.

'I tell you what, dearie. Why don't you pop along with your daughter now? An ambulance is out of the question, I'm afraid – we're having a very busy night, you see . . .'

'I see all right. I see perfectly. I shall indeed come to the hospital now – with my daughter. But let me tell you, if that baby of hers appears to have suffered in any way, I shall sue the hospital and the whole lot of you.' A particularly loud scream from next door forced her to finish quickly. 'We'll be there in ten minutes. Please, please make sure a midwife knows we're coming.' She slammed the phone down without waiting for a reply.

Peter, wearing just wellington boots and a mac over his

pyjamas drove them to the hospital. Robin lay groaning in the back: a very different Robin – in all respects – from the one who had lain there, giggly and tipsy, just six months previously. All the way there Alice shouted breathing instructions at her – more for something to do than because she believed it was making any difference.

· 33 ·

A Question of Confidence

'Don't worry darling,' whispered Alice, 'the doctor says it is quite normal.'

'What is – me or the baby?' Robin was lying with her face to the wall. She was sucking her finger – just as she had when she was a child.

'Now don't be silly. That it is utterly normal not to feel too euphoric at this stage. Especially when it was such a hard birth. Just stop worrying about it.' She tipped some cherries into a bowl and began plucking out the dead flowers from an enormous bunch in a vase beside the bed.

'You'll be home in a couple of days and then you'll feel better. You wait and see.'

As Robin did not seem inclined to talk, Alice dug her book out of her basket and sat down to wait for the next feed.

She did not have to wait long. The sound of a healthy pair of indignant lungs was soon to be heard approaching their door. Quite how penetrating the yell of a hungry child could be was something Alice had forgotten. It was frightening for any first-time mum, she thought, to cope with such desperate demands. She tried to give her daughter a reassuring smile, but Robin still had her eyes shut. Her face was pale – transparent, almost, in its whiteness.

'Here she comes – here let me give you a hand.'

'Mother, I can manage perfectly well on my own thank you. Undoing a nightie is about the one activity that causes me no pain . . .'

At that point the nurse marched into the room, carrying the puce-faced child in a no-nonsense sort of way.

'All ready are we then, dear?' Her voice was as starchy as her uniform.

She waited until Robin had arranged herself and then handed her the baby. She got a plastic bottle out of her pocket and put it on the bedside table.

'That's in case you find you don't have enough again.' She gave a crisp smile to Alice and left the room.

'Not exactly Florence Nightingale, is she?' said Robin, 'no wonder I'm feeling depressed.' She turned her attention back to the baby who, after a few nibbles, was refusing the breast. It started to cry again loudly.

Alice watched while Robin struggled. The temptation to interfere was enormous. The problem – she saw immediately – was a simple one: the baby's head was at the wrong angle for her to be able to suck comfortably.

'Mum, for God's sake give us some motherly advice could you?' said Robin at last. Alice, delighted to be asked, shifted the baby's position a little and clucked at it soothingly. The small person, when settled, soon lost itself to the task at hand, a look of adult concentration on its tiny pink face.

'Thanks. God, what a relief. Though I don't know why we don't just stick with bottles and have done with it. I never have enough anyway.' Her voice was sulky. 'It's such a palaver.'

'I can assure you preparing bottles is much more of a palaver than opening a couple of shirt buttons. I don't know how I'd have managed to keep an eye on Kate and Simon if I hadn't been able to breast-feed you for so many months. Besides, it's the most natural thing in the world.' A dreamy look came into her eyes as she watched the young mother and child.

It was precisely the 'natural' aspect of things that was getting Robin down so much. None of it felt natural. It felt messy, uncomfortable, difficult – but never natural. This had taken her by surprise. There had been unpleasant things about being pregnant – piles, toothaches, swollen ankles, sore back (Robin had had the lot) – but since she was having everything done for her, none of it had bothered her too much. Now, her problem was not really being so sore, but that she felt all wrong. She had presumed that giving birth would bring with it an immediate, instinctive sense of what to do next. That was how everyone had talked about it. As if becoming a mother automatically made you into one. What she was finding instead, was that the screwed-up little pink parcel was a baffling, alien creature, which she could hardly believe had come from her own insides. She had no idea what to do from one moment to the next. Nothing came naturally at all – except the desire to sleep and forget all about it.

As if following her thoughts, Alice said: 'It's all a question of confidence you know, darling . . . There, there, my sweetie . . . why not move on to the bottle now? . . . We are a hungry girl aren't we? My, my, my, we're going to grow big and strong . . . feel that grip, Robbie! Little iron fists we've got here . . .'

'Mum, would you mind giving her the bottle. I feel so tired.'

So Alice took the child and fed her. She had been dying to, anyway. After alternately de-burping and feeding the baby for a while, she noticed that Robin had not gone to sleep after all.

'Don't you think it's about time you settled on a name for her, darling? It seems such a shame to call one so beautiful "It" or "Fishface" all the time.' She kissed the child, who had now fallen asleep, on the tip of its miniature nose. 'She looks so like you did when you were born . . . what about one of your middle names?'

'Mother, you have already told me several hundred

times what you think my child should be called. And I have already told you that I loathe, positively loathe the name Clarissa. I have suffered enough putting it on forms all my life – I am not going to subject my daughter to a life of even worse torture.' The trouble was, she could not think of a single name that she really liked. There were lots that were passable; but none that she could imagine saying over and over again for the rest of her days without getting tired of it. The name problem sums it all up, she thought. I don't even have the confidence to give the wretched kid a name.

'Georgina. I have decided. Georgina. So now she has a name.'

'Oh darling, are you sure . . . The poor lamb will get called Georgie all the time, like that woman in that horrible film.'

'Honestly, Mum. You've been going on at me to make up my mind and when at last I do, you try and talk me out of it. Georgina is a lovely name.' But her voice lacked conviction. '"Georgie Girl". That was the film you're thinking of. But I'm not going to call her Georgie. It's Georgina.'

There was a knock at the door and Peter came in. After the standard round of inquiries as to the health of mother and child, Robin told him the name she had chosen.

Peter bent down over his tiny grandchild, still cradled in Alice's arms. 'Georgina, is it? My little Georgie? Georgie Porgie, eh? How sweet. What a pretty little girl we've got . . .' Alice looked at Robin; but she only sighed and turned her head to the wall.

· 34 ·

Some Kindly Advice

When Alice came to the hospital to take Robin and Georgina home, the starchy nurse ambushed her before she got to the room and informed her that the doctor would like a quick word. Alice did not like the doctor very much. Not that she doubted her abilities. It was just that she was a breed of woman with whom she simply could not feel at ease. Dr Winthrop's hobby-horses were women's rights and 'natural' medicine. These two causes found mutual expression in the campaign for a 'natural birth clinic' which she had been waging for several years. Alice, who associated such causes with Greenham Common and lentil soup, had nodded sympathetically to the history of local resistance, while secretly rejoicing at it.

Two large eyes, brimful with sincerity, now watched Alice over the top of small round gold spectacle-frames.

'I've spoken to Robin, of course – I believe in being absolutely frank with everybody. I've explained to her, as far as one can, why she is experiencing this depression and how she should fight it.'

'And how should she fight it, Doctor?'

'By relaxing, not forcing anything – by giving her mind and body time to come to terms with the shock of the birth. That was why I particularly wanted to have a quick chat with you Mrs Hatton, because you can help her enormously.'

Alice leaned forward expectantly, both hands clasping the handle of her handbag on her lap. 'I do so want to help,' she said.

'I know, I know.' The doctor's voice oozed understanding and warmth. 'The point is this, Mrs Hatton. Coming to terms with the baby – Georgina, isn't it? Lovely name – is something that she can only do on her own. She will need your help, of course – especially at the beginning. But the way you help,' she looked penetratingly into Alice's eyes, 'is vital. Confidence, Mrs Hatton. That is what Robin needs. In other words, any opportunity you get to give her confidence a boost – especially as regards the baby – then do it. Best of all if Robin doesn't realize you're doing it. Your daughter is rather insecure, you see – as a person I mean – and having the baby has brought it all to the fore.' She lowered her voice. 'The father having run off has not helped, of course . . .'

'He didn't run off, he . . . well never mind, it's a long story.'

'Yes, they always are,' sighed Dr Winthrop, as if she personally had been involved in hundreds of similar experiences. She cleared her throat.

'Anyway, I'm sure Robin is impatient to see the back of us. Lots of love and lots of rest, that's the answer. That way she'll gradually start managing – and wanting to manage – on her own. Soon she won't need you at all, you'll see.' She stood up and shook Alice energetically by the hand. 'Hopefully we can see the next one entering the world in more natural conditions . . .'

Yes, yes. Thank you for everything, Doctor,' said Alice and hurried out.

· 35 ·

Alice Helps Out

Robin ate so little that Alice got quite alarmed.

'You'll gradually lose the weight anyway, darling – there's no need to starve yourself,' she said, on several occasions. Every time, she met with the same sullen answer: 'But I'm not hungry.'

Indeed Robin seemed to have lost the will or desire to do anything but sleep. All the motions of looking after the baby were gone through – but always with Alice prompting, helping and ending up doing it herself. Such was Robin's apathy and lack of interest that Alice seriously believed that if she had not been there, Georgina would have spent most of her days half-starved and dirty. She tried to follow the doctor's advice, to find ways of getting Robin interested in doing things for her child, but the impenetrable, dream-like state of her daughter affected everything. In fact Alice found it hard not to get extremely angry with her. So many times she wanted to shout or hit her even – anything to provoke some sort of reaction from the dazed, sleepy face. Meanwhile, it was Alice's tread that Georgina waited for, Alice's rubbing that soothed the indigestion and Alice's arms that rocked her to sleep when some unknown terror or discomfort had set her crying. It always began with Robin trying, giving up and handing her over with a sigh, apparently too lethargic even to feel envious of her mother's abilities.

Perhaps it was the weather that finally did it. For one fresh, crisp autumn day, when Georgina was five months old, Robin astounded her parents by coming downstairs for breakfast. Alice, as usual, was in charge of the baby, who had long since had her morning bottle and was fast asleep in a wicker baby-cot that lived in the kitchen. More astonishing than Robin's first voluntary early appearance for months was how she looked. Instead of the usual big baggy shirt, over a pair of scruffy, loose jeans, she had on a pair of skin-tight blue corduroys and a soft blue and grey jumper with leg-of-mutton sleeves. So many months of picking at her food had reproduced the slim, trim lines of the old Robin. A few touches of make-up – which she had not worn since the New Year's Eve dinner nearly a year before – completed the transformation.

'Well, well!' exclaimed Peter and gave her a kiss.

Alice too was dumbfounded: 'But Robbie, look how thin you've got . . .'

'I know. Isn't it marvellous?' she said, smiling and doing a small twirl. 'I can't tell you how glad I am. It just suddenly came to me this morning that I was probably the right shape for some of my old clothes. They feel good too.'

Over the next few months, Robin's transformation continued. Like a butterfly emerging from its chrysalis, she began showing all the colours of her old self: the smiles, energy, confidence – all the components that had made up the character of the Hatton's youngest daughter before her disastrous sortie to Birmingham.

These changes appeared to bear no relation to the baby at all. Robin was assembling her own armour against the world. It left no room or strength for coping with anyone else. Besides, there was always Alice to deal with Georgina for her. The only one who said anything on the subject was Peter – and then only to Alice. He did not dare to upset Robin now that she was so obviously on the road to recovery.

196

'It's not right, Alice,' he said, on more than one occasion. 'I know I never got that involved with the baby side of things, but anyone can see she ought to be taking more interest in Georgina.'

Alice was sitting in the middle of the sofa, knitting. Strewn all around her were different coloured balls of wool, funny-shaped needles, tape-measures, and pattern books. She had just embarked on a delightful, but very complicated all-in-one suit for her granddaughter. The background colour was blue and dotted all over it were going to be tiny farmyard animals. Little pom-poms were supposed to go round the ankles and wrists, but she wasn't sure she would bother with those. In the last few months she had become rounder and rosier. As she sat on the sofa, peering over her glasses at her knitting and brushing away the small wisps of grey hair that kept falling over her face, she looked the very picture of grandmotherly contentment. Anyone suggesting that just eighteen months ago this lady had been dying of love and unrequited passion, would have been laughed out of town.

'It's early days yet, Peter darling. Don't be such a fuss-pot,' she said, still absorbed in her knitting. 'You know what Dr Winthrop said. That it will all take time.'

'But it's been over eight months now. And look at her.'

'Look at who, darling?' Alice was not really listening.

'Alice, for goodness sake don't be so infuriating. Look at Robin of course. There's nothing wrong with her at all now and yet she gives that poor little blighter about two seconds of her attention per day.'

'You don't know that, Peter. You're not here during the day.' Alice put down her knitting and began studying the pattern again. It really was extremely complicated.

'Well it's obvious. All those aerobics and things she goes to. Acting classes – I thought she'd done with all those years ago.'

'She's getting back into the swing of things. You have to

if you want to keep up in that world, she says. And I can believe it.'

They were sitting having this conversation after a quiet dinner together. Robin was out for the evening – another practice which she had taken to recently – although quite who with they were not sure. It was so difficult to ask without sounding nagging or prudish.

'Well she's going to have to recognize that she's got a child to look after sometime,' he went on huffily.

'But I don't see what there is to worry about.' Alice now put down the pattern book and looked at her husband properly. 'She's got us to help with the baby.'

'You, you mean.'

'Well me, then. We're a joint baby-sitting team though, aren't we?' She smiled at him.

'Alice . . .' He knew he was about to enter dangerous waters. 'Are you sure that we're not making it too easy for her? I mean, you don't think that perhaps you help her so much that she feels there's nothing left for her to do?' His apprehension was well-founded.

'I don't know how you can say such a thing, Peter. You know what the doctor said – to help her as much as I can, to let her relax and find herself again. As far as I can see that is exactly what is happening. Anyway, you don't see what goes on during the day. I give Robin every opportunity I can to do things for Georgina. I really do.' She picked up her knitting again. The clicking needles sounded angry.

In fact Alice was not being totally truthful. During the first month or so she had indeed tried to get Robin to do things for the baby. Inevitably, however, a routine had slowly established itself. A routine that was now very firmly fixed, and which basically involved Alice doing everything. 'What the doctor said' had actually become 'what Alice wanted to remember of what the doctor said.'

· 36 ·

Plans for the Future

Being good or evil is often something that happens accidentally, rather than being a premeditated, heart-tussling decision. That Peter, for instance, had become an altogether 'better' person and certainly a more zealous husband had been almost totally the result of coincidental circumstances. He had been in the right place and the right frame of mind at the right time. Outside events, beyond his control, had jerked his life into a new rhythm that he could never have foreseen or thought up for himself.

So it was with Alice. She never sat down and decided to be unfaithful to her husband. Just as she never planned, consciously, to try and keep Georgina for herself. Such a notion would have appalled her by its wickedness. The idea simply grew on its own, forced out of circumstances.

After an early trip to the supermarket one morning – having left Robin and the baby asleep – Alice let herself into the house by the back door. She was lugging several bags of shopping and wanted to dump everything straight onto the kitchen table. Before unpacking she decided to go upstairs and check on Georgina. The child was showing signs of a nasty cough and had woken up several times during the night. It was only when she passed out of the kitchen and into the hall that she heard sounds of

199

merriment coming from the lounge. Curious, she opened the door slightly and peered in. Mother and child were too absorbed to notice. Robin was kneeling on the floor, over a squealing, delighted Georgina, who was kicking her chunky legs in appreciation of the game. The two were bathed in the shafts of sunlight that poured in through the french windows leading on to the back garden. Any natural pangs of jealousy that Alice might have had were magnified into something far more serious by what Robin was actually saying to her daughter – or rather half-saying, half-singing, as she tickled the fat little tummy between phrases:

'And Mummy's got a joooob . . . and it's in New Yoooooork . . . and Georgina's coming toooooo . . . just me and youuuuuu . . .'

'Robin!' Poor Robin got such a shock that she jabbed her fingers quite hard into Georgina's midriff and made her cry.

'God, mother, you gave me a fright. How long have you been standing there?'

'Long enough,' said Alice grimly, scooping the child off the floor. 'She needs changing – I'll do it,' she said, and turned towards the door.

'So I suppose you heard about my plans, then?' said Robin sharply, still kneeling on the floor, plucking tufts out of the carpet. 'You must have done, I suppose, since you were standing there spying on us.'

'Don't you dare talk to me like that, Robin. I won't have it. I was there for only a few seconds. But yes, I did hear. I couldn't very well help it.' With that Alice whisked Georgina out of the sitting room and upstairs to the nursery. The nappy in fact did not need changing at all, but the action at least gave her time to think. Although to refer to the desperate scrabbling of Alice's mind as thought, is perhaps generous. Instinct – the drive for self-preservation – was the only impulse to take command of her racing thoughts, and it was this instinct that immediately produced one solid conviction: she could not lose the child now. Not since her own children had been small had Alice been so happy, so fulfilled. Georgina was even more enjoyable, in a way, because she had been unexpected and because she had arrived at a time when Alice's life had been without hope. Now the baby was her life. With the baby she could cope with anything. Feeling fond of Peter – even putting up with his new fervent love-making, (though still in the dark), were burdens easily born when she could sense, although not quite hear, the calm, regular rhythm of the breathing child next door. That she was a grandmother, that the lines round her mouth and eyes were getting crinklier, that ugly little veins had started to burst in her legs – none of these things mattered any more. She did not mind the whole decrepit business of growing old, of living with a man she did not love, so long as she had that small object, whom she did love desperately, living with her.

The words of the doctor which had really etched themselves upon her mind – although she hardly knew it – were: 'She'll start managing – and want to manage – on her own. Soon she won't need you at all, you'll see.' Somewhere hovering in the shadows of her consciousness, Alice knew she had deliberately fought the fulfilment of those words; she had made it as difficult as she could for Robin to get close to her baby. Yes, there had been plenty of opportunities for Robin to do things for Georgina, but never without Alice standing there in the background, hovering, watching. She had never just handed over completely and let Robin have a go at getting on with it. She knew that, with such a professional audience, Robin, in her weak state, would always end up giving in and asking Alice to do it. She told herself and Peter that she had tried. But really she had done exactly the opposite. So all the scrambling thoughts upstairs resulted in a single icy-clear resolve: Robin could go to America. But if it was with Georgina, it would be over Alice's dead body.

As she had shown several times in the recent past, Alice was more than capable of rising to a crisis.

'I didn't mean to shout at you, darling,' she said gently when she came back downstairs; 'I was just surprised, that's all. You've never said anything about any plans to go to America. Well, not recently, anyway.'

'I didn't say anything because it has only just become a real possibility again,' replied Robin, pleased to see that her mother had decided to be sensible.

'So what's happened?' said Alice, taking up her knitting, looking as nonchalant as possible.

'Well, you remember that girl I told you about who was working in New York and who said she could help me before?' Robin's voice was now eager and excited. Alice nodded. 'She's in England at the moment – just for two weeks holiday – and I met up with her a couple of nights ago and we got talking and well, you know, the idea just grew and grew. Apparently she works for a small rep company – a good one, though – who are always keen for people with English accents. Incredible, isn't it? I mean she says I could just walk into a job there, no problem at all.'

'It does sound marvellous, I must say. Now that I've got over the initial shock I really think it might be rather a splendid idea. You've got Simon just down the road, after all.'

'Oh Mum, don't be silly. Chicago is miles away. The last reason I'd go would be because of silly old Simon. I'm sure he'd say the same about me if it was him . . .'

'Robin, I was joking,' she put in quickly. 'I think a fresh start is probably just what you need – right away from where you've been so unhappy.' The more Alice thought about it, the more she realized that it really would be much more satisfying to have Georgina completely to herself. This bombshell could actually turn out to be a real blessing.

'And you'll want to take Georgina with you, of course.'

202

'Yes, of course,' replied Robin, in a much quieter voice.

'What about accommodation and that sort of thing? Does your friend – what's her name? . . .'

'Mickey. Well Michele actually. But everyone calls her Mickey.'

'Yes, well, this Mickey then. Does she have a place you can stay?'

'Yes, yes she does.' The eagerness was back in her voice. 'A flat – I don't know where exactly – which she shares with a couple of girls, and I think there's a bloke there too.'

'Sounds very jolly, I must say.'

'I think it would be fabulous. New York! Just think of it.' She flung her arms wide as if literally embracing the prospect.

'None of the others in the flat have children, I suppose?'

'Oh no, I don't think so. But Mickey says it will be fine – that they all love kids.'

'Are baby-minders cheap over there?'

'Baby-minders? Well, to be honest, I hadn't really thought about it. I mean I don't think I'd need one; with so many in the house, there's bound to be someone staying in when the rest are out. Isn't there?'

Alice did not say anything. She must play her hand carefully this time. All she wanted to do was to sow some seeds of doubt in her daughter's enthusiasm.

'Obviously there are a few details I've still got to sort out,' Robin went on defensively, 'but it's the first idea that has really appealed to me in months.'

'And I think it is a wonderful idea. I really do. I'm sure we can work something out. Let's talk to Dad about it tonight.'

'That reminds me. I've invited Mickey round for a drink tonight. I hope you don't mind. I wanted her to meet Georgina – and you and Dad of course.'

Alice was taken aback. Mainly because, even before going to Birmingham, Robin had seldom brought any of her friends home. It must mean she really is intent on this project, she thought. And a single butterfly took one wild jump in her stomach. To have Georgina . . .

'I don't mind at all. Not to meet the person with whom you're going to share the next phase of your life and career?' she said teasingly, 'it would be unthinkable.'

· 37 ·

Meeting Mickey

'It sounds a hare-brained scheme if you ask me,' was Peter's response to the idea. He had spent the best part of the day trying to negotiate his early retirement. The rest of the partners were putting up a lot more resistance than he had anticipated. It was rather flattering in a way. On the other hand they were putting him under considerable pressure to change his mind. It was all rather trying. He wanted very much to talk to Alice about it, but held off so that when he finally told her, it would be a big surprise. As soon as he stepped inside the door, she had thrown this crazy idea of Robin's at him, so it would have been a bad moment to confide his plans anyway. He thought it was high time that Robin and Georgina moved out of Quadrant Grove, but packing up for America was not exactly what he had had in mind.

'Why can't she join some rep company in London? Why go traipsing all the way to the States, for God's sake?'

'She says that there aren't any jobs here; whereas she's virtually guaranteed one over there.'

'I've heard that before.'

'I must say, darling, that I actually think it is rather a good idea.' She went on quickly before he could interrupt. 'She really has had such a hard time here in the last couple of years, I think a complete break would work wonders.'

'I can't believe this, Alice.' He stared at her in amazement. 'I would have thought you would be the last person to go along with such a mad plan. What about Georgina, for a start? It doesn't sound the sort of life that would be exactly conducive to bringing up a baby, does it?'

'I'm sure something can be worked out,' said Alice quietly. 'No doubt we shall discover more shortly. Robin is at this moment meeting the mysterious Mickey off a train and bringing her home for a drink.'

'Really? How improbable.' The prospect of a peaceful evening now well and truly shattered, Peter drained his first whisky and went for the second. As he did so, the front door banged shut.

'That will be them,' said Alice, getting up and automatically straightening her skirt and patting her hair.

'Mickey, this is my Mum and Dad. Mum, Dad, this is Mickey. Georgina's upstairs, of course. I'll get her in a second.' Everybody was embarrassed. However, Mickey was not the sort of girl who could stand silences for long.

'Well hi everybody! Delighted, I'm sure. Wow, what a great pad you've got here. I mean really cool. You never said, Rob. You never said that you were kitted out here in the lap of luxury. This is just great.' She bounced down on to the sofa.

Mickey looked even younger than Robin. Her hair was blonde, with two streaks of red at the front that kept falling across her eyes. When she bothered – about every three minutes or so – to push this energetic fringe back off her face, she revealed two very large green eyes; it looked as though a child had tried to draw round them with a bright green crayon and got bored half way through. Every protruding part of her flesh was covered with trinkets, leather thongs, bangles, bells, and chains. Neck, ears, fingers, wrists, ankles and toes: every inch had its own little decoration. She made what Alice had always called Robin's 'arty' way of dressing look positively middle-aged.

'Would you like a drink?' asked Peter, aware of his daughter's eyes pleading with him to be nice.

'I guess I would. Thank you very much. I'll have a dry martini and gin on the rocks – with a slice of lime, if I may.'

'You may indeed,' said Peter with a gallant smile, 'except for the slice of lime, that is. Would lemon do instead?'

'Why sure. Lemon's great. I forgot. You guys don't go in for limes over here, do you?'

For Robin's sake, both Alice and Peter were on their best behaviour.

'I know it sounds silly, but I didn't realize you were American Mickey. Robin never said,' remarked Alice, smiling kindly at her daughter's friend.

'You never said?' Mickey gave Robin, who had sat down next to her, a playful prod in the ribs. 'Why that's the most important thing about me!'

Robin just laughed. 'Honestly, Mum, I thought it was obvious. Here, have a peanut, Mick, to make up for it.' Peter had surpassed himself in the kitchen by finding not only a fresh lemon, but a half-empty packet of peanuts as well.

'So you want to whisk our daughter off to the wild west, eh?' began Peter.

'The wild east you mean,' said Mickey, with a hint of annoyance. She was bright enough to know when someone was trying to patronize her.

'And do you really think it will be that easy for Robin to get the sort of job she wants there?' asked Alice.

'Mrs Hatton, it is a cinch. Believe me. I've been doing rep over there for five years now – and I know the scene. Those guys are just crying out for types like Rob. With an English accent and her looks she's got it made. You're going to get rich, baby.' She grinned at Robin, who smiled back, looking embarrassed and pleased.

'It all sounds so vague, that's my worry, Mickey,' said Peter, trying to sound concerned in an open-minded, non-boring sort of way. 'With Georgina to take into

207

account, we are quite keen to know as much as we can. I'm sure you understand. It's not that we don't believe you or don't trust you.'

'Oh yeah, the baby!' squealed Mickey, as if she had forgotten all about its existence. 'Let's have a look. Go on and get her, Rob – I'm just dying to meet your daughter.' This, for some reason, struck the American as hilarious. Robin cuffed her as she got up from the sofa, still looking awkward but happy.

'Do you want me to fetch her, darling?' asked Alice. 'Then you three can carry on talking.'

'Oh, OK. Thanks, Mum,' said Robin, as if it was an exception rather than the rule for her mother to take charge of the child.

It had not been that long since Alice had bathed Georgina and put her down for the night. Her face was still glowing pink from the bath and she had not yet dropped off to sleep. She was lying on her tummy, her second finger in her mouth, blinking at a large teddy bear that was painted on the inside of her cot.

'Hello there my angel . . . Hello my lamb. Not asleep? Clever girl. Did you know we were having visitors, then? Come along . . . there we are.' Alice picked her up and held her close, luxuriating in that distinct, warm baby smell of cleanliness, milk and fresh linen. She wrapped a soft white blanket over the pink night-suit and carried the precious bundle downstairs.

At the sitting room door, Robin seized her daughter, wanting to show her off to her friend herself.

'Georgina Clarissa Hatton, meet Mickey Schiffries.'

'Oh wow, Rob, she is beautiful. Hey there, little girl,' said Mickey, patting Georgina on the head, 'and how are you doing today?' Perhaps aware that they were all looking at her, she added 'oh hell, I never know what to say to babies. But she's great, Rob. I love her.'

'Go on, hold her for a second,' said Robin offering the child to Mickey.

'Oh my God, no. I mean, thanks Rob, but they always start crying and puking on me, if you know what I mean.' She retreated to the sofa and lit a cigarette.

Mickey did not stay very much longer. By the time Alice had taken Georgina back upstairs and patted her back till the eyelids had started drooping, their guest was refusing a second drink and saying she had to go.

'So soon? I am sorry. Delighted to have met you Mickey. Perhaps you can come again before going back to New York?' said Alice.

'I might just do that. Thank you for the drink.'

'I'll help you find a taxi,' said Robin, grabbing a jacket and bustling Mickey out of the house. After the door slammed, they could hear peals of laughter from the two girls.

'Well!' said Peter, throwing himself into a chair, 'I think that settles that.'

'What settles what?' said Alice.

'Well you cannot seriously think that Robin should put herself in the hands of that . . . that . . . creature, can you? The idea is preposterous.'

'I don't see anything wrong with it at all. You're the one who's always telling me I should accept that the children have got to be independent. There's nothing wrong with Mickey – a little reckless maybe. But I can well believe this thing about pretty English actresses being highly sought after. And that's the main thing after all – the job.'

'Alice, I cannot believe I am hearing correctly. You want to agree to post our daughter off to what is probably some white-slave-trade, drug-trafficking den in New York, with a baby in tow to boot?'

Alice actually laughed. 'Peter darling, don't get so carried away. Mickey was not that bad. And the flat is in Greenwich Village, she said, which is supposed to be very nice. As for the baby, I agree with you there. It would be ridiculous for Georgina to go too.' There, she had said it. She had got it out at last. Her plan. She had been dreading his response; but she was saved from it by the banging of the front door for the third time that evening.

'Got a taxi straight away,' called Robin from the hall. She burst into the sitting room. 'Well? What did you think? A bit trendier than me isn't she? But a real sweetie, I promise.' She picked up her half-drunk gin and tonic from the coffee table and looked from one parent to the other.

'It seems,' said Peter slowly, 'that your mother and I hold rather different views on the whole subject.'

Robin looked at her father.

'Well go on then, let's hear it – I'm dying of suspense here.'

'Shall we talk about it over some supper?' suggested Alice sweetly . . . 'It's all ready. Just a quiche and some salad I'm afraid; but I put a nice bottle of white wine in the fridge to go with it.'

They filed into the kitchen, like three suspects walking into court to hear their sentence. The cold meal was already spread out on the table. While Alice cut the quiche, Robin was despatched to get some wine glasses and Peter dealt with the bottle. When at last they were all sitting down, Alice plunged in.

'Your father does not think going to America is a very good idea Robin . . .'

'Alice, for goodness sake . . .' She knew it was an unfair way to start, but she wanted to push Robin into believing that Peter was against her. That way, she would be more likely to agree with any suggestion of hers. They were crude tactics, but Alice had long since resigned herself to playing dirty. It was her only chance of winning.

Peter glared at his wife. 'I have never tried to stop you doing anything you really wanted to, now have I, Robbie?' he began. His daughter, intent on pushing a small piece of bacon through an assault course of chopped tomatoes and lettuce, only nodded. So he pressed on.

'It is just that I am not sure how reliable your friend Mickey is . . .'

'Dad, honestly,' she burst out, 'you've only met her for a few flipping minutes . . .'

'I know, I know, I know,' he held up his arms in mock surrender. 'First impressions aren't everything. But they are something. And in this case they weren't – for me at least,' he shot an accusing glance at Alice – 'altogether favourable.'

'You should see her on the stage,' said Robin sulkily, 'then you'd think differently. Of course she's a bit scatter-brained – and so am I for that matter – and very . . . well, very American I suppose. But she's a bloody brilliant actress. She's streets ahead of anyone else I've ever worked with. She can really help me, Dad, I know she can. Go on, Mum, you're on my side. Help me explain,' and she turned to Alice with beseeching eyes.

'I don't know about being on anyone's side,' said Alice cautiously, 'nor of being able to persuade your father of anything he does not believe is right.' I must come to it gradually, she told herself. She got up and started scraping plates as she talked.

'I do know, however, that this chance you have in America sounds wonderful; that it sounds altogether too wonderful to pass up. If it all works out – as you and Mickey seem to believe it will – then it really could make your career.' She did not dare look at Peter. Robin was listening to every word, drinking in the encouragement, as Alice meant her to.

'Oh Mum, you do understand, you really do . . .'

'But . . .' The word hovered in the air. Was she really brave enough to go through with it, she wondered? But she only hesitated for a moment. When she spoke, her voice was firm and confident. 'But I do not think that you should take Georgina with you.' Robin carried on staring at her. Peter picked up the pepper mill and began studying it closely.

'I know that, as yet, we don't know very much. But we do know that it is a flat, that four other people live there, that

211

there are no other small children and that your hours are bound to be unpredictable. Mickey, although I thought she seemed a very sweet girl' – here she did steal a glance at Peter, who was still fiddling furiously with the pepper mill – 'did not strike me as a natural baby-person, if you know what I mean.'

Robin took a long deep breath and stood up from the table. 'I'm going outside for some air,' she said.

Alice cleared away the remaining plates in silence. Peter hardly moved. She put a bowl of fruit salad and a small jug of cream on the table and pushed them towards him.

'Help yourself, dear,' she said.

'I don't know what to say, Alice. I really don't. I simply cannot understand what you are playing at. How can you possibly want Robin to go off to America with that girl?' The question came from the heart. He really did not understand. Something did not quite fit, but he could not put his finger on it. He had no inkling of what was really in his wife's mind.

'For exactly the reasons I told Robin. I think it is a fabulous opportunity for her. It's a challenge. It will do her good, even if she comes back with her tail between her legs in a few months' time.'

'But Georgina . . .'

'As for Georgina, it would clearly be very unsuitable to have a baby in tow over there, so she can stay here, with her grandparents.' Alice smiled. The picture of innocence and good intentions.

'But, to be brutally honest, Alice, do we really want to be shackled with a baby? I mean, we've done that bit, haven't we? We're due for some time to ourselves.' He toyed with the idea of telling her of his new retirement plans, but thought better of it. Once again, it just was not the right moment.

'Of course we should always be there to help Robin when she needs us – I'm not denying that. And you, especially, have really helped her with Georgina. But she's not a baby anymore – Robin, that is. She's got to accept the responsibility for what's happened sooner or later. And I think now is the time. I'm perfectly happy to lend the child money. But so that she can move to her own place in London – with her own daughter – not so that she can go gallivanting off to New York, leaving us holding the baby, so to speak.' He smiled in spite of himself.

'Well, let's see what comes of her think in the garden,' said Alice, wishing she could have some telepathic control over her daughter's decision.

A few minutes later they heard Robin come in and go upstairs.

'Probably best to leave her, don't you think?'

'Yes, probably. I've got the final proofs on my book to go through anyway. I'll be in the study.'

Alice washed up and put the untouched fruit salad back into the fridge. Then she went into the sitting room, where she put a good two hours in on Georgina's jump-suit before going up to bed.

· 38 ·

All For Alice

Soon after Peter had left for work the next morning, Robin came downstairs in her dressing gown looking tired and dishevelled. She found Alice dusting the sitting room. In a large play-pen in the corner, Georgina was working off her breakfast by throwing all her toys from one corner of the pen to the other; then crawling over to them and repeating the exercise.

Robin threw herself on to the sofa and started flipping through Alice's book of knitting patterns.

'Did you sleep well, darling?' said Alice, knowing the answer.

'Lousily, thank you.' She threw down the book. 'I can't go, Mum. I've decided. I just can't. It wouldn't be right – either to take Georgina or not to take her. I'd feel so bloody guilty all the time. And if I did take her I probably wouldn't know how to look after her properly anyway – I'd probably kill her or something. Oh God, what a bloody mess I am.' Alice, who had sat down opposite her, wondered if she was going to cry. She deliberately did not interrupt, wanting Robin to say everything she had been tossing over during the night, before she played her final hand.

Robin swallowed the lump in her throat and went on with a rueful grin: 'I wouldn't want an American brat on my hands anyway. London's a much nicer place for a child to grow up in . . .' There she dried up, sounding unconvinced and miserable. Alice stepped in to the rescue.

'I couldn't agree more.' She leant forward in her chair. 'But Robin, there is no need to talk about feeling guilty if you take this chance to go to the States. Why feel guilty when you can leave her in the loving hands of her grandparents – who aren't that old yet! – where you can be absolutely sure she's all right? You'll know so much about how she's getting along that it will be almost like being with her yourself. No, don't say anything. Let me finish. I think it's one of the strengths of a good family that they can help each other out, cover for each other when it is necessary. I know this is a bit different, because it means you going away, but the principle is the same. And goodness me, it's not as if it has to be forever!'

Robin no longer appeared to want to interrupt and Alice began to worry whether she had overdone it. Then a new and brilliantly persuasive argument came to mind. 'One reason I feel so strongly about this, Robbie,' she said, with an air of confidentiality, 'so strongly that it has possibly surprised you a little – is because I want to see you take those opportunities that I never had when I was your age.' The idea blossomed as she warmed to her theme. 'I'm not saying I was not happy and lucky to settle down straight away with a husband and children – I've had a very special life – but I really had no choice. Women of my generation generally didn't. Whereas you do. It would be silly to let Georgina take that choice – and this opportunity – away from you. You'd only grow up to resent her for it. With us in the equation, to look after her while you are away, you can have the best of both worlds. You can make a go of your acting and have your child brought up in the family – as close to you as she can get, without actually being under the same roof. I'll say it for the last time, Robbie. I think you should do it. And I don't think you'll ever be truly happy unless you do it.' She sat back exhausted, but very pleased. It had gone much better than she would have imagined

215

possible. Even so, she was taken aback by Robin's explosive reaction to her words. She leapt from the sofa into her mother's lap, threw her arms round her, half-sobbing, half-laughing – Alice was not sure which – into her shoulder. She patted her daughter's back and made comforting sounds, as if she was the baby, not Georgina. Alice was still unsure whether she had triumphed or failed. Then Robin pulled herself up, wiped away the tears with the back of her hands and shook the hair out of her eyes. She looked steadily at her mother. For a second Alice was scared that she would read the true motives behind her arguments. But all she said was:

'I'm not sure I really understand it. Or rather I don't really understand how you seem to understand it so well. But you've made me see that I can do this wonderful, selfish thing, without having to die of guilt over it. You've made me see that . . . well never mind . . . you know it all, anyway.' Even then Alice dared not be absolutely sure of what Robin meant.

'You'll help me explain it all to Dad, won't you? You're so good at explaining things. And he really did seem so set against the idea. I'm going to ring Mickey now and tell her to count me in.' She sprung out of the room, without even a glance at the play-pen, where Georgina, worn out from the toy-chucking game, was asleep on her tummy.

Alice walked quietly over to where the child lay. Looking down at the tiny figure, her delight passed through her in waves. She wanted to weep with joy, with the relief that comes after victory or when a great danger has passed. Robin's venture to the States would, she was sure – she hoped, anyway – last for a couple of years at least. The longer she was away, the less likely she would ever be to come back and try to claim her daughter for her own. Peter could write his books, live at the office, lock himself in his study – she did not care a straw. As for Edward, she humphed in scorn at the thought of him. If he came crawling through the door with a bunch of roses and two one-way tickets to the Bahamas she would laugh in his face. She did not need him now. She did not need anyone now. Because she had won the darling child for herself. And the child would need her – every minute of every day for years.

'Clarissa, my pet,' she murmured, 'my sweet lamb. You belong to me now, my love. I'm here to look after you. And I'll always be here.'

She felt the springs of a new life stirring within her; like all the raw elation of childbirth with none of the pain.